paper
covers
rock

paper covers rock

Jenny Hubbard

EMBER

Text copyright © 2011 by Jenny Hubbard
Cover photograph copyright © 2011 by Andrea Chu

All rights reserved. Published in the United States by Ember, an imprint of Random House Children's Books, a division of Random House, Inc., New York. Originally published in hardcover in the United States by Delacorte Press, an imprint of Random House Children's Books, New York, in 2011.

Ember and the colophon are trademarks of Random House, Inc.

Visit us on the Web! randomhouse.com/teens
Educators and librarians, for a variety of teaching tools,
visit us at randomhouse.com/teachers

The Library of Congress has cataloged the hardcover edition of this work as follows:
Hubbard, Jenny.
Paper covers rock / Jenny Hubbard. — 1st ed.   p.   cm.
Summary: In 1982 Buncombe County, North Carolina, sixteen-year-old Alex Stromm writes of the aftermath of the accidental drowning of a friend, as his English teacher reaches out to him while he and a fellow boarding school student try to cover things up.
ISBN 978-0-385-74055-5 (hc : alk. paper) — ISBN 978-0-375-98954-4 (glb : alk. paper) — ISBN 978-0-375-89942-3 (ebook) [1. Conduct of life—Fiction. 2. Death—Fiction. 3. Boarding schools—Fiction. 4. Schools—Fiction. 5. North Carolina—History—Fiction.] I. Title.
PZ7.H8583Pap 2011   [Fic]—dc22   2010023462

ISBN 978-0-385-74056-2 (tr. pbk.)

RL: 6.0

Printed in the United States of America
10 9 8 7 6 5 4 3 2 1
First Ember Edition 2012

To the steadfast shepherds of the second floor—
Ted Blain, Ben Hale, Tom Parker, and John Reimers

The title is the writer's stamp of approval.

—ANONYMOUS

Call me Is Male.

When my dad gave me this journal two years ago and said "Fill it with your impressions," I imagine he had a more idyllic portrait of boarding school life in mind. I imagine he pictured a lot of bright things, sending his only child to an institution whose official motto is *Ad Lux*. But these pages have remained blank. I have not had much to say until now—when now is everything.

If you are reading this, you have happened upon it by accident. Call me Is Male.

My apologies to Herman Melville, from whom I may have to steal a few words to tell the story that is about to be told, that is in the middle of being told, that will never stop being told. Such is the nature of guilt; such is the nature of truth. But it is also the nature of guilt to sideline the truth.

Welcome to the sidelines, Dear Reader.

If you get bored with my literary efforts, with the plot or characters, if you find that good ol' Is Male is putting you to sleep, read a real novel, a Great American one. Read *Moby-Dick*. Read to your heart's content. Though if you are a reader, the heart is never content.

Newspapers may tell you the plot, but they never tell you the real story. And they never, ever tell you what started the whole thing to begin with. But when the end is death, maybe what comes before doesn't matter. What happens on September 30 is still going to happen.

So, what happens?

1. The bell rings at exactly 11:45. I have been waiting for this bell. I own a watch just so I can set it to Birch School time, just so I can know exactly when this Saturday bell, the one that dismisses us from six days of classes in a row, will ring. The Birch School, like all boys' boarding schools, is timeless; time drags on forever here, which makes the bell mean something.

2. I leave the classroom for the dining hall and eat lunch. (Not worth elaborating on—sorry boys'-school food.)

3. I go back to my room to change clothes. (We all wear blazers and ties to class.) My room feels depressing at this time of day, when I am normally in class during the week. The carpet looks like it hasn't been replaced in twenty years because it probably hasn't, and in the corner near my closet, some other guy who had this room before left cigarette burns that I have never noticed until this moment. My roommate, Clay, hasn't made his bed (typical), and a half-eaten bag of Doritos sags near his pillow.

4. I start down the hill to the river by myself at approximately 12:30, but my friend Thomas catches up with

me. We arrive at the designated meeting spot at approximately 12:50. No sign yet of Glenn and Clay, so Thomas asks me a question: "Do you remember what it is that makes the sky blue?" Because on this day, the sky is bluer than it has ever been.

"I think it has something to do with the spectrum of light and the nitrogen in the atmosphere absorbing all of the other colors except blue," I say.

"It's weird to think about living under a green sky, or a red one."

I agree.

Thomas says, "Blue is the right color for it, that's for sure."

I say, "I always thought it was weird to think about how you're under the same exact sky as some kid in China who has no idea that you exist, and you have no idea that he exists, only that there has got to be at least one kid in China looking at the sky right now."

"Isn't it night over there, though?"

"Yeah, but there still has to be some Chinese kid looking at it."

"Maybe he's counting stars," says Thomas. "Did you used to do that?"

I did.

Thomas says, "I wonder why we don't do that anymore."

This is our last real conversation, verbatim. Every conversation you will find in this book I am writing is verbatim. There may be a comma where the speaker intended for there to be a semicolon, but other than that, my journal/Not-So-Great American Novel is entirely accurate. Even though I haven't

3

slept for two nights in a row, what you see scrawled throughout this journal that my dad gave me is real. I am big on verbatim because I am big on truth. Truth: as important and essential as rain.

(copied verbatim, punctuation and all, from the newspaper in the library)
Death Notice, Raleigh *News & Observer*,
October 2, 1982

Thomas Edward Broughton, Jr., 17, of Raleigh, died September 30 as the result of a swimming accident in Buncombe County, NC. Thomas, a junior at the Birch School, was a member of the varsity football and track teams and a good friend to all who knew him there. He was born September 21, 1965, in Raleigh, where he was a member of Christ Episcopal Church. He spent the summer volunteering at the Boys Club, an organization for underprivileged youth, while working toward becoming an Eagle Scout. Thomas is survived by his loving parents, Thomas Edward Broughton, Sr., and Grace Banes Broughton, and by his younger brother, Trenton Banes Broughton, all of Raleigh; by his grandmother Lucy Elvington Broughton, also of Raleigh; by his grandparents Mr. and Mrs. Hendricks Folsom Banes of Oxford, Mississippi; and by various aunts and uncles and cousins in Raleigh and elsewhere. A service in celebration of Thomas's life will be held at Christ Episcopal on Friday, October 6, at 11:00 a.m., to be followed by a private burial. In lieu of flowers, dona-

tions can be made in Thomas's memory to the Boys
Club of Raleigh, P.O. Box 957, Raleigh, NC, 27607.

Rock, Paper, Scissors

After the accident, Thomas's body is carried up to the infirmary on a stretcher, and the whole time Glenn and I are sitting on the bench outside, I'm picturing Thomas's drowned
body inside, wrapped in towels. Mr. Armstrong, the Headmaster, and Dean Mansfield, the disciplinarian, question us
out on the porch so that we don't get the infirmary furniture
wet. Glenn and I both know enough to let Glenn do the talking because he is athletic, popular, smart—prefect material—
and I am not. I am what is thought of at Birch as a Good,
Solid Kid, one of many. Glenn is thought of as a Golden Boy,
one of a few.

Dean Mansfield tosses up question number one like a
tennis lob, and Golden Boy delivers it neatly back into the
Dean's court: "We told Thomas everything we knew about
jumping from the rock, not that we've done it that many
times ourselves, but, yes, we have done it before, haven't we,
Alex?"

Good, Solid Kid nods his head, and Golden Boy contin-
ues. "Teenagers take risks, Mr. Mansfield; that is part of
growing up. A person doesn't grow if he doesn't take risks."

"That is true, Mr. Everson, but the seed of risk does not
always grow into a straight trunk. The tree can rise crookedly
out of the ground."

"Yes, sir," Golden Boy and Solid Kid say in unison.

"You hold in your hands the opportunity to tell the truth
about what happened at the river," Mr. Armstrong says.

"Yes, sir," says Golden Boy.

"Yes, sir," says Solid Kid.

"You, the students, are the caretakers of the Birch School Code of Honor," says Mr. Armstrong. "It is your code, not mine. Do you understand me, boys?"

Yes sir yes sir yes sir yes sirree Bob. We are, like most of our peers, unfailingly pragmatic. If the school finds out we've been drinking, we'll be kicked out, no questions asked, and the call will be made to our parents, who will have to stop whatever it is they are doing, hop into the car, and make the winding ride across the mountains to take us home. So Glenn and I do what most any other boy in our shoes would do: we lie.

I lie to my dad, too, over the office phone that Dean Mansfield lets me use while I stare at the poster on the back of Dean Mansfield's closed door. "Character: Build It," it says in red capital letters that arch, rainbowlike, over a kid standing by a pile of bricks. My dad wants to come right then and check on me, but seeing as he is currently in Maine on sabbatical from his university professorship, that proves difficult. I convince Dad that I'm okay, that I will be okay. I call my mother, too, but she isn't home, and I begin to worry that if the school reaches her first, she will drive down, unannounced, from Potomac, Maryland, where she lives with her boyfriend, a man named Victor with thick white hair. So I call my dad back and ask him to call his ex-wife. He says that he will.

My dad is good that way—responsible to a fault, calm in crisis—and whatever goodness I have is because of him. He had been a boy who, if presented with a pile of bricks, would have built a tall tower—not a fort, but something that made you thoughtful, that lent you foresight. If someone had given my mother a pile of bricks, she would have thrown them at every window she could find, delighted at the drama of breaking glass.

If I were good the way my dad is good, then I wouldn't be filling up these pages. They would be blank, the way they were when I came to Birch. Tabula rasa. They would be clean, the way I used to be.

I belong in a janitor's closet, which is where I hide after I change out of my wet clothes and call my dad. As you might expect, the janitor's closet is full of cleaning supplies. I unwrap a roll of paper towels and a spray bottle of I-don't-know-what, spray the I-don't-know-what onto the paper towels, strip down to my boxers, and clean myself, over and over, sixteen times, one time for every year I have lived. I use up two rolls and the whole bottle of spray, and although my skin is burning, I am still not clean. Out, out, damned spot. I am running scared; I am curled into a ball in the dark; I am as far away from the sky as I could possibly be.

Until it has scared you with its endlessness, sky is just sky.

These are all landsmen; of week days pent up in lath and plaster—tied to counters, nailed to benches, clinched to desks.

TUESDAY, OCTOBER 3, 1982, 9:05 P.M.

Hide-and-Seek (a Leitmotif)

Someone is going to pop around a corner and scream, "You're it!" That is why this particular landsman is clinched to a desk in the Samuel E. Walter IV Memorial Library, his face hiding behind a large novel about a dead whale. He is the proverbial "it." The sentence at the top of the page is from the first chapter of said novel, which seems to fit the moment, which is why Is Male records it faithfully, strange punctuation and all. He has never kept a journal before, but his father has kept them for years, noting the time, date, and location.

Is Male does not need to note the location: the location is the library because the dorm is not safe. Is Male cannot do anything, doesn't want to do anything, except watch the black ink of his pen roll over the white page. So he might as well do his homework for English—see the rough draft for yourself. By the way, Is Male has a big crush on his teacher.

Alex Stromm
English 500
Ms. Dovecott
10/03/82

What I Carry

I carry a backpack full of things I'm not supposed to have, a pack of cigarettes and a tattered *Playboy* magazine—adult things that speak of the burden of adolescence and of the line we have to walk between childhood and adulthood. Parents and teachers expect us to be both. Besides my backpack, I carry a fishing pole. So do my friends Thomas and Glenn because that's why we're headed to the river, to swim and maybe catch some bass. I don't know why, though, because we always throw them back.

What I carry are simple things that you could find on any Birch School boy at any given time. I think about the things that I could have carried to the river instead, my Latin reader, for example, but I come here to escape school. Or I could have brought a sweatshirt, but cold water on skin, like the cigarettes, makes me feel real again. The students here think that they are missing out on the exciting lives that their friends back home are living. People in our hometowns think we were sent off to boarding school because we are discipline problems or drug addicts or just bad kids with bad genes. "What else could their parents do with them?" they probably say to each other.

That is not how my parents felt about sending me here. They wanted to give me brothers; they wanted to give me the opportunity to try things I wouldn't have tried at home. What I carry, too, is the burden of proof that they were, in fact, right. That I am coming to know who I am. I now run cross-country, I have more endurance and drive than I knew that I had, and I also have friends, good friends. But one of these good friends is dead, and so I carry his life, and his death, inside me, too. I was close to him when he lived, and I was close to him when he died. I don't think my mom or dad ever expected this kind of closeness.

What I carry in my backpack down to the river, I carry not knowing that in less than an hour Thomas Broughton will be dead. That is not a knowledge I carry yet, but I will carry it soon—the knowledge of my darkest self—and I will carry it forever.

Landsmen, Soldiers

After Thomas dies, everything seems outlined with electricity as if the school is at attention, poised for war. The boxwoods along the brick sidewalks appear taller, topped with a hundred little eyes. Even the lampposts look as if they are conspiring. Guys who have barely shown their faces for two whole years are wide-eyed, wide-mouthed, flushed as if with fever. They huddle on the grass outside the classroom buildings and whisper, jerking their heads around to make sure the enemy doesn't creep up on them. And who is the enemy, other than the element of surprise? I can't believe it myself, and I was there: Thomas Broughton, dead nine days after his seventeenth birthday.

But even death does not stop the Birch School schedule. Sunday, the first of October—for most guys, a day of rest; for me and Glenn, a day in hell, filled with interrogation (to be

10

detailed later, once I can stomach the reliving of it) and the beginning of sorrow. No matter how sad or sick or angry or wounded any of us here are, everything (as in: *life*) marches forward as planned. That is the Birch way. So on Monday morning, we all go to class.

What I Think About on the Way to English

I am the only one here who knows that Thomas lost his virginity to Kelly Somebody-or-Other, a girl he met at the beach on the Fourth of July. I know so much about it that it feels like my own loss, but in any boy's case, it's not loss, is it? It is gain, big gain, one of the biggest gains, if not *the* biggest gain, in the journey to manhood. So here is how Thomas does it, and I admire him mightily for it. He says to Kelly, who has just handed him a beer, "If I drink this, will you take advantage of me?"

According to Thomas, Kelly looks like Farrah Fawcett with dark hair, which she tosses around as she answers with a question: "In what way?"

"In the way I want you to," says Thomas, and she smiles at him with all of her teeth to let him know that he is right.

Does Kelly know now that the boy who touched her is dead?

What I Think About in the Hall Outside English

Thomas had an irrational fear of squirrels (which I made merciless fun of him for). . . . One winter night during our sophomore year, Thomas and I took a taxi all the way into town just to eat Chinese food. We gorged ourselves, and he paid for it, both the cab fare and the meal, and afterward, back in his room, we listened to Steely Dan albums. Thomas owned every single one. Thomas will never hear "Reelin' in the Years" again. . . . Thomas will never again steer himself across these sidewalks, never again move like the rest of us, hard-faced as the bricks beneath our feet, without peripheral vision, back to our dorms, to the post office, to class, going through the motions. . . . The two of us when we hardly knew each other, sitting in Mr. Parkes's freshman English class our very first week at Birch. Our homework had been to read "The Lottery," a short story about this town that stoned to death one citizen a year simply because it had always been done. The discussion afterward wasn't about plot or structure or boring stuff like that; it was about traditions—what role they played in civil societies and all that—and Thomas and I talked afterward about how cool Mr. Parkes was not to force his opinions on us like teachers at our old schools back home. . . . I can still read, but Thomas's eyes are closed.

In English Class, Part One

In I walk, my head bowed, my books packed neatly in my L.L.Bean backpack. We all have L.L.Bean backpacks, just as we all have L.L.Bean sweaters and L.L.Bean moccasins. We are interchangeable, and because I am of average height (5' 10"), though a bit on the thin side for a sixteen-year-old, I've gotten used to guys on my hall borrowing my clothes. It will get sorted out in June, when we have to pack up again.

If I am still here in June. If I don't get found out. I am playing it cool. Playing it cool when I feel as uncool as I have ever felt in my entire life.

It is everyone's first class of the day. Mine just happens to be English. Miss Dovecott tells us we can lay our heads on our desks or stand at the windows and stare at the trees. We all feel how Thomas is not here with us. His desk is full of empty.

"Do you want to talk about it," she says, "or ask questions?" Some of the guys look over at me or Glenn expectantly, but most of them drop their heads into their hands.

"I guess we could all use some quiet time," she says. She returns to her desk and lays her head down on it, hoping we will take her lead. We don't. Her shoulders move up and down slightly with her breathing. She has great shoulders.

Rock, Paper, Scissors

5. At 1:00, Glenn and Clay arrive, and my dear ol' roomie pulls the fifth of vodka, which he has been hiding in his closet for weeks, out of his backpack. We all pass it around until it is half empty. The leaves, with the last of their green, filter the sun. That thin thread of sun is the only thing that finds us. We are deep in the woods on the last day of September.

6. This next move is Clay's idea. His father had a club when he was a student here in the 1950s, and, according to Mr. Claybrook, the initiation for the club required its members to jump into the French Broad River from the high rock. Which three of us have done before and one of us hasn't.

7. Glenn tells Thomas, "You have to jump out far. Jump, not dive. Got it?"

8. Thomas says, "Got it," and drinks vodka with the rest of us.

9. The four of us walk to the rock.

10. The rock is exposed, like we all are about to be.

11. Glenn says he'll go first, to show Thomas how it's done.

12. Thomas says, "Okay, but I'm not scared."
13. Thomas takes another chug of vodka.
13. Thomas takes another chug of vodka.
13. Thomas takes another chug of vodka.

In English Class, Part Two

I'm still staring at her shoulders when, at 8:16 a.m., Miss Dovecott rises, walks to the chalkboard, and erases it from top to bottom, from side to side, wiping out every remnant of word, every stray comma. By the time she turns back to us, Joe Bonnin has fallen asleep. Some guys laugh, but none of us do anything to stir him, so Miss Dovecott walks over and shakes Joe's shoulder. He doesn't wake up, so she has to shake him again. That's when Glenn and I catch eyes, understanding. Miss Dovecott is afraid, afraid to touch him. By the time she returns to the front of the room, her armpits are wet, and it is the thing that draws me out of myself, the thing that calms me down: the realization that a teacher could be more scared than the students—and scared *of* the students.

"Under the circumstances," Miss Dovecott says, "I think it only fair that I give you an extra day on the essay that was due today, and I'll talk now about the story you'll be reading tonight." Some of us reach into our backpacks and pull out our books. On any other day she would require us to hold the text, as she calls it, in front of us and take notes in the margins, but today, she says nothing. Time hulks over us. Miss Dovecott plays with her watch, takes it off her wrist, and swings it gently from side to side. I study it; it looks old-timey. I try to hypnotize myself.

Out the window a robin keeps returning to an unsteady

branch. What is the robin looking for, its head ticking around, its black eyes blinking? Why doesn't it chirp?

I want to hear something other than the inside of my head, something other than Miss Dovecott rambling on about the story. "Let us say, then, that Miss Emily represents the South, the pre–Civil War South, so if she is on this end of the spectrum"—and at this point Miss Dovecott draws a straight line across the smooth board, labeling one end "Emily"—"then who is on the other end?"

She doesn't slow down for an answer because we haven't read the story yet. A couple of guys turn their notebooks sideways and draw the line across the page. "Homer," she says. "Homer Barron, the healthy, hearty Yankee whom Miss Emily—daughter of the Confederate South—poisons."

"She *poisons* him?" Joe Bonnin, now awake, asks.

"Why?" says Auggie van Dorn, who looks like a Cabbage Patch doll. "Was he mean to her or something?"

"No," says Miss Dovecott. "You'll have to read the story tonight and find out for yourself."

"What kind of poison does she use?" asks Jovan Davis, a black kid from Atlanta.

"Rat poison," Miss Dovecott answers.

I look at Glenn; he looks at me.

"Does she sprinkle it on his dinner or something?" Joe is clearly intrigued by this whole poison thing.

"Glenn," says Miss Dovecott, "do you happen to know how poison might be best administered?"

"No, ma'am." He is staring at his hands, which are flat on the desk, palms down.

Joe clears his throat. "Glenn was with Thomas," he says.

15

"I know that," she says to Joe, but she is looking at Glenn, and when he looks up, some inexplicable electric knowledge passes between them.

Glenn Albright Everson, III, Class of 1984

Glenn is the sort of guy other guys respect. For one reason, he doesn't make excuses for himself, but most of the time he doesn't need to: he earned a perfect score in math on the PSAT. Glenn is a top scholar and all-conference athlete. Glenn does not argue with adults as some students do; I think it's because he doesn't want to be that involved with them. He is the most self-reliant guy I know; he does things his way, and that works out for him 99 percent of the time. He doesn't seek the spotlight, yet it finds him. Thomas wanted to be Glenn's best friend, but Glenn doesn't play those kinds of girl games.

Alexander Stromm, No Middle Name, No Roman Numerals, Class of 1984

Alex is rarely in the spotlight, and that's the way he likes it, though he wishes he were funnier because at Birch, funny is revered, funny is cool. Alex is a good audience for other guys' jokes, and other guys seek him out to tell him jokes because he is appreciative and he has a great laugh that makes a weird little dimple in his lower right cheek. Alex stays out of the spotlight by being Above Average, except in math. Numbers don't make sense to him even when you turn them into letters like "x" and "y." He has learned that if you don't talk much in class, the other guys think you are either really smart or really dumb, and so when he knows he can answer a question correctly, he raises his hand, but no more than once per class period, because then he would be in the spotlight.

In English Class, Part Three

"Alex was with Thomas, too," Auggie says, unnecessarily, because the students, the teachers, everyone, knows who was where on Saturday at approximately two o'clock in the afternoon. I want to shoot Auggie a dirty look, but I'm lying low. Besides, how do you shoot a dirty look? Do you take out your eyeballs and pocket them into a slingshot, and pull back the rubber band, and . . .

Miss Dovecott is gazing at me, and I forget all about my eyeballs. To her credit, she does not tell the class that she was there at the river that day, too. Our screams led her there.

"I'm sorry for your loss," she says. "For *our* loss," she corrects herself, glancing over at the oxymoronic desk, the one full of emptiness.

Postscript

Even though other boys in other classes sit in that desk, I expect Miss Dovecott to remove it, to store it in the attic or something, but the next morning, Thomas's desk is still there. In other classrooms, too—history, chemistry, pre-calc, Spanish—there are still desks.

Are the green fields gone?

Yes, Mr. Melville, they are gone, *long* gone, which is why I must sit here in this library and write about them, just as you did before me. Your novel is art. My novel is the sloppy work of a guy trying to fill up a journal with inadequate words.

Green Fields

Now and *then* are two opposite places, two different time zones. *Then* was a lifetime ago. Then, I ate that lunch. Then, I rhymed my poems. Our first homework assignment in fifth-form English (pretentious boarding-school speak for eleventh grade) was to write a poem that evoked the mood of autumn. Here is mine, copied here for posterity, now that the green fields are gone.

> *The geese are on the wing,*
> *And cold has settled sternly,*

18

A moon mocks its own low calling,
I wrap my throat in yearning

For a song no longer mine.
Where had it gone, that tune?
I once sang it soft and fine;
it rang of crystal June

when I had basked and dipped
and thrown the fishes back,
and daylight didn't slip,
and dreams were true as fact.

But now there's only sand
and water shrunk with dread,
and nothing I had planned
still strums inside my head.

By Alex Stromm
9/4/82

An eerily foreshadowy effort that Miss Dovecott chose to read out loud to the class the day I turned it in. After she did, I was out in the open, I was someone with a name, and I knew I would be called a few other names once I returned to the dorm that afternoon. For a second, I was mad at her. And then she wrote some of my poem on the board, underlining words, and I think that's when I fell in love, though it didn't feel like falling. She asked us questions about diction and placement, the same as she had done the day before with poems by actual writers. It's difficult to put into words on a page, but before this moment, I was not actual, or not full, or full of shit. Miss Dovecott made me real.

"The poet chose to leave this untitled," she said, making it seem as if I'd done the exact right thing. "But if it were your poem, if you had weighed your choices and ended here, what would you call it?"

She made us write our titles on scrap paper—"To keep you honest," she said—and then she circled the room with her lilting voice, pecking the board with chalk as we, one by one, offered up our ideas. The title she liked best was "Sand," which connotes a desert, the opposite of a garden, cradle of paradise. But contrary to the sentiment contained within my waltzing stanzas, I felt—for the first time at Birch—a future rising up inside me.

And then she turned to the board and erased, and wrote another boy's words across the dust left behind by my poem.

But that was *then*, before the accident. Miss Dovecott— without whose existence the filling of these pages would not be possible; without whose existence this story would remain untold. I am in love with Miss Dovecott. And she might, just might, be in love with me. She writes about me in her journal the same way I write about her in mine. At least I dream she does.

If you think about it, it's kind of weird that Miss Dovecott would sign on for a job here. A young Yankee female in an age-old Southern male institution. Even English-teacher bookworms need friends and bars. The campus is more beautiful to adults than it is to us: we see it as a fishbowl, and they see it as a nest, with the stone buildings tucked inside the

20

rolling hills at the feet of the Blue Ridge Mountains, supposedly the oldest chain of mountains in the United States. To
adults, old is cozy. To us, old is something we can't imagine
we will ever be.

Miss Dovecott isn't old; she's right out of college, probably twenty-two, maybe only twenty-one. My father says he
admires the Birch faculty because they give so much of themselves to the place—seven days a week, twenty-four hours a
day. Of course he's aware of the free housing and food they
receive in addition to a teacher's salary, but that doesn't com-
pensate for a lack of privacy and time to themselves. He
could never work here, he says, and I certainly haven't encouraged him to apply.

I have seen Miss Dovecott talking with Mr. Parkes, my
advisor. Sometimes they sit together at lunch, but it doesn't
look like love, except for the fact that when they talk, she
plays with her watch and smiles. Maybe they drink wine together at his apartment. Maybe they read poems and stories
out loud to each other.

Scissors Cut Paper

Poems and stories: NOT the newspaper version of things.
There is a boarding school version of things, too, and it's like
the newspaper version, only more deliberate. The boarding
school version, sent out ASAP in a letter written by the
Headmaster's secretary and signed by the Headmaster, is
there to soothe the parents, who pay shitloads of money to
send their sons away. The letter is sent so that, even in the
wake of disaster, parents will keep sending their sons to, and

21

I quote, "a community who makes it not a business but a moral duty, an obligation, to prepare boys for life." My dad bought into this, literally and figuratively.

My dad calls me several times on the day of the accident, the last day of September, after he receives a call from Mr. Armstrong. (Later in the week, he receives his own personal copy of the soothing letter.) There are three messages tacked to my door, scribbled in sloppy handwriting, when I return to the dorm Saturday night after holing up in the janitor's closet. The last note says to call my dad no matter how late, but by that time, the school switchboard is closed, so I get permission from my prefect, a senior I'll call Bob Dylan (just because I can), to use the pay phone in the gym. Glenn wants to go with me, but Bob Dylan won't let him because it's after check-in.

The basement of the gym, night or day, is like a dungeon and smells worse than one. Dad answers on the first ring.

"I'm not going to lie to you," I say, lying. "I'm not fine right this minute, but I will be."

"I'm coming to get you."

"No, Dad, please. Everything is under control. You know this place. It's like the army. They don't let anything slide, least of all a potentially troubled young man such as myself."

My dad tells me he's talked with Mr. Armstrong and Mr. Parkes, but he still isn't sure that in loco parentis is the proper modus operandi. "The first flight I can get out of here is Monday morning."

"Don't waste your money, Dad."

"Then will you call me tomorrow and the day after that and the day after that? If I'm not in, keep trying. Better yet,

22

call me as soon as you wake up. That way, I know I'll be here."

I tell him I will, but I do not tell him that I won't be sleeping tonight, tomorrow night, or probably ever. Before I leave the gym, I grope my way to the corner bench in front of my locker, put my head in my hands, and cry myself a river. When I get back to the dorm, I check in with Bob Dylan, who offers me a fatherly pat on the back.

Clay Claybrook: not fatherly. Not brotherly. Hardly human. I got stuck with him. Thomas and I had planned to room together, but then Glenn's chosen roommate got kicked out at the very end of our sophomore year for stealing another guy's Coke out of the dormitory refrigerator. Birch has a strict code of honor—no lying, no cheating, no stealing, and no second chances—so Claybrook, otherwise known as Gaybrook, got assigned to him. When Glenn found out, he asked Thomas if he wanted to switch, and Thomas said yes, basically screwing me over. Thomas explained that he had asked Glenn first, in the spring of our sophomore year before the Coke incident, but that I had been his next choice.

Good, Solid Kids don't mind playing second fiddle to Golden Boys. Golden Boys have it hard, too. One false move gone public and not only do you lose your chance at prefect, but you are out of here. When it comes to honor, Birch doesn't believe in second chances. Which is why it is a good thing that Clay left the river before the jumping began and took his bottle of vodka with him, which is why Miss Dovecott didn't see it when she came on the scene. Clay left because of something Thomas said. Clay is a very touchy guy.

When I come back to the dorm after talking to my dad, Glenn is sitting on Clay's bed. Clay is in the bathroom.

"You've been crying," Glenn says.

"I don't want to talk about this right now," I say.

"Thomas's parents came by after chapel and took some of his stuff home with them."

"What about the rest of his stuff?"

"Dean Mansfield told them he'd box it up and save it for some scholarship kid," Glenn says. "His mom stayed at the hospital with the body. They're doing an autopsy."

"Why?"

"It's what they do when they need to rule out foul play! They're going to find the alcohol! We are dead, Alex! Dead!"

"No, Glenn, we're not. We're alive. Thomas is dead."

He stops and looks at me. "Do you not realize what is about to happen here?"

"Yeah. But maybe we deserve it."

"We do not deserve it, Stromm. Thomas was shit-faced. If he'd listened to us and jumped out like we told him, he'd still be alive."

"Are you saying it's his own fault he's dead?"

"No, of course not. I'm saying it was his choice to chug half a pint of vodka."

"We could have stopped him," I say.

"He would have done it anyway," says Glenn.

"How do you know?"

"Because I know Thomas."

"Well, I knew him better than you," I say, "and I have my doubts."

Glenn rises from the bed with a funny look on his face.

"What?" I say.

"I just figured out a way for us to stay, me and you. Even if they do find alcohol in his bloodstream—"

"Which they will—"

"I figured it out, Stromm. We're safe."

Just then, Clay opens the door and kind of shoves me out of his way.

"I was just leaving," Glenn says. "Let's all try to get some sleep, okay?"

Green Fields Gone

There is always more to the story. Look around at the books on these shelves: stories, stories, stories, get your stories here! Stories within stories that lead to other stories that lead to other stories. A whole Pandora's box of stories. And then, of course, there is the story of how stories collide—the fiction and the fact—and the very fine line between them.

Rock Beats Scissors

Outside the infirmary, the two boys sit side by side on a bench, a hard wooden one with slats, and in the stone-cold clarity of the moment, with the haze of the vodka shocked out of his system, one of the boys thinks about the rectangle of wood underneath him, one that was made by a man he did not know, from some tree that used to live in a forest, and how that craftsman could never, in his wildest dreams, have imagined that the most important moment in these two boys' lives would take place on wood that he had hewn and sanded. The sun begins to lower itself behind the mountains, and the shadows on the lawn outside the school infirmary become fingers, broad, giant fingers, creeping up the backs of the Dean of Students and the Headmaster, who inform the boys that the Buncombe County Sheriff's Department, now that it has drawn up an official accident report, has decided to leave any further investigating to the school.

The two boys are escorted by the Dean of Students, first back to the dorm to change clothes, and then to the main building, where the school's offices are, so that the boys can call home to the people known as parents, who gave them life. One of the boys will sit in an office and stare at a poster that mocks all that his father has tried to teach him; one of the boys will hide out in a janitor's closet and try to pretend that what just happened didn't really happen.

Green Fields Long Gone

Like I said, more to the story: there is another bench outside the Headmaster's office, to which Glenn and I are summoned Sunday morning October 1, less than twenty-four hours after the accident. Dean Mansfield finds me in the library, writing in this journal, and I stuff it into my backpack, and he leads me to where Glenn is waiting outside. We are directed across the misty quadrangle. The morning fog has not yet lifted. How symbolic, I think.

Dean Mansfield walks behind us so that we can't talk to each other, and I get the feeling that our days of talking are numbered. Mr. Armstrong's office door is closed. Dean Mansfield knocks and tells me and Glenn to wait in the hall, and on the bench between us he places a tape recorder and presses the On button.

I look at Glenn. Without a word, he grabs me by the shoulders just as he did the night he found me in the janitor's closet. I was very, very clean when he found me, but I was shaking, and Glenn had to grab me. "Stromm," he said, "get ahold of yourself."

I almost laughed, it was so cliché, but it was then that Glenn convinced me that the proverbial *they* would come after us. And of course, Glenn was right. Guys like Glenn know all the places another guy might hide. Guys like Glenn don't make mistakes.

Addendum to the Birch School Handbook, October 1982

Let it be known that the large granite rock at the head-waters of the French Broad River is off limits to every Birch School student. Climbing upon or jumping from this rock is a dismissible offense. As with other dismissible offenses, there are no second chances.

Scissors Cut Paper

An announcement regarding this addendum to the rules is made in chapel that same night, October 1, at a school-wide memorial service for Thomas. Thomas's parents and little brother are still here. I do not want to see them, so two hours before the service, I go for a run to get in my miles for the weekend, even though I know Mr. Wellfleet would be understanding if I didn't. I run seven miles of hills, above and beyond the required four. So it is easy afterward to make myself vomit, which I do, and then I check myself into the

27

infirmary. When you're sick, you're not allowed on dorm. I make myself vomit again for good measure once I'm there so that I can stay with Nurse Patty overnight.

I would rather stay with Miss Dovecott. Her apartment is in the infirmary, not on dorm like the male teachers' apartments. This old school doesn't know what to do with her, now that they have her, Miss Dovecott fresh out of Princeton. Birch gets a hard-on for Ivies. I would rather stay with her, but I'm guessing that would be a dismissible offense.

No one at the school has a crush on Nurse Patty. She is sugary and plump, like a gumdrop. If you want to have a crush on a Birch bitch (a long-standing label, not of my invention), you don't have a lot of options. You've got your dining-hall employees, but they're inbred, being from the nearby hollers, which is also kind of where I'm from, just farther away. I'm not really into mountain lasses, even though they are nice and I went to school with some of them before I came to Birch. There's Mrs. Davido, the French teacher, who is undeniably beautiful for an older lady, and if you could imagine her twenty years younger, you could develop a crush pretty easily, but who wants to work that hard? Plus, she is married to Mr. Davido, who teaches Spanish, and it's creepy to think of them together in bed. And Mrs. Inskeep, the switchboard operator, has a face as leathery as an orange. They are like grandmothers and, like grandmothers, would do anything for us. They are there to serve, and we are there to take.

Miss Dovecott isn't like that. Hemingway or Fitzgerald would be able to describe her better than I can: think Brett Ashley without the royal pedigree, or a kinder, gentler Jordan

28

Baker. Miss Dovecott is dark (like me), and good-looking in a tomboyish, no-nonsense way. Her face isn't beautiful, because her nose is kind of big, but when she smiles, which isn't all that often, her face looks like a sunburst. It's blinding. She's got great legs, slender, well-defined. Soccer legs. She played attack on her college team, a fact that gives her way more credibility with us than an Ivy League degree. Half of the school has a crush on her, and not just because she is basically the only female under the age of thirty within nineteen miles.

Miss Dovecott isn't like the other women, because she is both giver and taker. She has given me my raison d'être. She has cut out my *coeur*, now cradled in her hands. *Mon Dieu*. I lie on this cot where other sick boys have lain and drown a thousand times over in my nightmares.

Green Fields

In the days after Miss Dovecott read my poem in class, a whole new vista of knowledge spread out before me, and life on dorm became much less interesting than life in English class, than life inside my head. Who cared if I could hear Clay jacking off every night? I could rise above it; I was learning how to float across the horizontal lines that I'd always thought were reasonable borders. My running times began to improve because, all of a sudden, I could make the trail beneath my feet disappear, and the destination was nothing more than a wide-open space of beginning. One night, the guys across the hall found a "Coloreds Only" sign in the attic of our dorm and plotted to hang it over the table in the dining hall where the ten or so black students at Birch sit at lunch, and the next morning when they were at breakfast, I snuck into their room, stole the sign, stuffed it into my backpack, and walked over to the maintenance shed, where I borrowed some black paint and covered up the "lor." "Coeds Only." I returned the sign to their room, and they never said anything about it. I was beginning to see *through* things; language was flying at me from all directions, and I grabbed on to it as if it were the tail of a kite.

Meditation and water are wedded for ever.

SATURDAY, OCTOBER 7, 1982, 3:13 P.M.

You're getting the picture, aren't you, that Is Male is scared out of his mind? Which is why he spends hours surrounded by the order of the Dewey decimal system, writing his Not-So-Great American Novel. If your trusty narrator were a little less intimidated by the permanence of ink, you might well be reading an autobiography, one that doesn't steal its chapter titles from sentences written by a guy named *Her*-man.

Thomas's Funeral

For six days, the flag in front of the main building flies at half-mast. On Friday, October 6, the student body crosses the state in buses for the funeral in Raleigh, a much bigger deal than the memorial service I chickened out of. For most of us, it is our first funeral, and we shuffle and bow, uncomfortable with the postures of grief. And for what are we grieving? For me, it is so much more than loss of life.

Because when I see Thomas's parents and little brother at the funeral, my soul weaves a nest into some inner part of me I never knew existed. Although I'm not sure what Melville meant by it, somehow it feels right: meditation and water *are* wedded forever, and the church is out of proportion to the world. I offer my seat to an old woman and inch to the back wall, as far away as I can get from where Thomas's family and the casket (closed) are.

The Casket

Polished wood the color of autumn. It is extremely difficult to convince myself that Thomas is really in there. What if he isn't dead; what if he hears all of this in his brain, but his mouth doesn't work? Or his feet or hands? What if he can hear, and he is just playing a joke on all of us?

Hands

Make a fist, Thomas. Make a fist and punch through the lid. Arise like Frankenstein. Mummy-walk to the back of the church where I am and beat me to a pulp. I hold hands with myself to keep from shaking, remembering the cold of your hand the one time I held it. Remember, Thomas? Remember how at Birch, it's always either too hot or too cold? Remember how our freshman year it snowed the first of May, two whole feet?

Before we left the river, after Glenn found you under the murk and he and I pulled you to shore, after we tried CPR and mouth-to-mouth again and again, even though it was stupid and pointless, I held your hand.

It doesn't matter what the minister says as he stands over your shiny casket; it doesn't matter that everyone but me in this church is singing. What idiot chose "I've Got Peace Like a River" to be sung at your funeral? Is this part of the joke, too?

In the back of the church, I think about your last words to me and the last words you heard, which were mine: "Rock, paper, scissors." I mouth these words to the tune of the hymn while it groans out of the organ, and the syllables scan. But your last syllables to me don't scan, and why should they? Normal people don't go around talking in iambs. Your little brother, Trenton, seems to agree; he is nodding his head in time to the music, each downbeat like a peck at the truth.

Rock, Paper, Scissors

We all take chances with our lives. It is all such a gamble. I learn while I'm sitting on that bench outside the Headmaster's office less than twenty-four hours after Thomas died that I may be safe. Because the tape recorder is there between us, Glenn tells me the good news by reaching into my backpack and writing on a sheet of paper that he tears out of the back of my journal. I don't think he realizes what it is, but in spite of what I just said at the start of this paragraph, I'm not taking any chances. From now on, my Not-So-Great American Novel is staying in the library.

I've taped the torn page back into my journal.

> *Game plan—Clay is going to take the fall. He's in there right now swearing to God that he and Thomas were the only ones drinking. So swear the same thing.*

33

Why in the world . . . ?!
Because I told him I'd tell the whole school what Thomas said.
He'd rather be dismissed than outed?
Hell, yeah. Can you blame him?
No.

And I couldn't. There was no worse label at an all-boys' school than "gay." It was worse than leprosy, way worse. If someone laid that name on me, I would want to leave, too. Worse than "liar," worse than "cheat," worse than "thief." Getting kicked out for drinking was even considered "cool" in some people's books. (Not mine, but some people's.) It doesn't even surprise me that Clay said nothing about it the night before as we lay there on our very separate twin beds. When Clay comes out of the office, the look on his face tells me that Glenn wasn't kidding. "Don't worry, Stromm," Clay whispers. "I wouldn't touch you with a ten-foot pole."

Peace like a River (Ha, Ha)

For how long was I one with the water? It's a math problem I give to myself while being interrogated inside the Headmaster's office after Clay has taken the fall. Clay is going home today, but where are you, Thomas? The autopsy came back on your body. You were way over the limit of what's known as "legally drunk," but I guess you probably know that. *Knew* that.

"If the water was cold, Mr. Stromm, as it typically is at the end of September, then why did you want to swim in it?"

Thanks to Golden Boy, who is still waiting with the tape

recorder on the bench in the hall, I am prepared with the prologue to the accident that we agreed to the night before. "We were playing this game of Frisbee, kind of like tag, where we . . ." As I explain the made-up game, I picture the orange Frisbee under Clay's bed, and then I picture those cigarette burns in the carpet, made by some other asshole who smoked like a chimney and probably got away with it. "And we got hot from all the running around, so we went for a quick dip, and that's when we decided, stupidly, to jump off the rock."

Dean Mansfield takes over for Mr. Armstrong. "Did you have a taste, or more than a taste, of vodka?" he asks, enunciating every word.

I know that with Glenn, Dean Mansfield will not have time to repeat the question. I know how Glenn will answer: "No, sir, no way. Coach Harding would kill me for drinking." Glenn is the star wide receiver, well on his way to setting a school record for receptions.

But when Dean Mansfield asks me, I pause, questioning how effective the licorice gum was that Glenn slipped out of his backpack on the way up the hill as we followed Thomas's stretched-out body. They probably could have broken me if they'd tried a little harder.

"Mr. Stromm?" Mr. Armstrong turns his grandfather eyes on me. "Had you been drinking before you jumped from the rock?"

I have already told so many lies that it almost feels like truth when I answer, "No, sir."

Ten seconds at the most, mathematically speaking; that's how long I was in the water before I knew something was

35

wrong. My last ten seconds of innocence, you might say. For ten seconds, I *was* the river.

Reverend Black

Birch School's own personal shepherd, Reverend Black, goes with us to the funeral, driving the lead bus. We are shuttled back to school, back across the state, that same day, Friday. When I descend the bus steps, I have to grab on to the rail put there for the old and crippled.

Reverend Black is waiting at the foot of the steps. He has something he'd like to say to me. I don't have anything I'd like to say to him, but I'm not going to make a scene, even though it means being alone with him in his office, a narrow room under the chapel, a room that is hard to breathe in, like a coffin, because it has no windows.

The good reverend is light in his loafers. The good reverend is a hypocrite. He preaches on the sin of homosexuality—at least once a trimester, he quotes the Scripture, twists it so that it fits his message.

His Message

Leviticus 18:22, the King James Version: *"Thou shalt not lie with mankind, as with womankind: it is abomination."*

Now, I'm no stellar grammarian, but to me, it sounds like Leviticus is saying that we really shouldn't be lying with anybody.

The good reverend says that we are made in God's image. God is perfect. *Therefore,* God is not gay. *If* you engage in the sin of homosexuality, *then* you will contract gay cancer and die a very slow, very painful death.

I'm no stellar mathematician, either, but I'm pretty sure the reverend's logic wouldn't hold much water in Mr. Behr's geometry class.

None of us trusts the good reverend as far as we can throw him. Which wouldn't be far, because he is a chunky man, overstuffed like a worn-out armchair.

I should tell Reverend Black that I'd rather have this talk with my advisor, Mr. Parkes, because I like the way Mr. Parkes talks, kind of old-fashioned. And he never rambles on or repeats himself like so many other teachers. He knows when to stop. The good reverend does not, and now he is telling me that I will have to sit here and listen to his bullshit once a week, otherwise known as "grief counseling," which Glenn will also have to endure. "On occasion," says Reverend Black, "you two might even like to come in together." As I sit there at one end of his black leather couch, a brass lamp cold at my elbow, Reverend Black perches at the other, his left palm flat on the cushion between us. He wears a gold signet ring on his pinky. I don't trust men who wear rings. (Wedding bands don't count.) The rumor is that he had Jesus Christ's initials inscribed on it, but the engraving is too swirly for me to confirm or deny that rumor, and I am not about to lean in closer to inspect it.

A Fine Young Man

"Alex," he begins, "you are a fine young man." I almost start laughing. How many times have I heard that before? A million at least. And what meaning of "fine" does he intend here? I put my hand over my mouth, that's how close I am to cracking up. Because he thinks I am about to cry, he hands me a box of tissues. To keep from having to explain myself, and to be polite, I take one and kind of swipe at my eyes with it.

"Alex, you're a fine young man, and we at Birch want you to know that we support you in your time of struggle. We are here for you, and God is here for you. If you don't own a Bible, then I'd be happy to lend you one."

I lie and say that I do.

"I think you will find solace in some of the Psalms and in the book of Job."

"Isn't he the one with all the patience?" I ask, to play along. If I play along, maybe I won't have to come back. I am very good at playing along; it is one of my talents.

"Yes, yes, he was." Reverend Black seems pleased and asks if I remember Job from religion class, which is required of all third-formers. I confess that I don't, but I tell him I went to Sunday school as a child, a lie that comes out of nowhere. Why would I lie about that and tell the truth about not remembering his class? I am starting to sound like Holden Caulfield, and that does not make me happy, because he is just about my least favorite character in all of American literature.

The Rainbow Connection

"You will come to learn that God shows us His mercy in small ways. You may be walking along thinking about Thomas, for example, and up in the sky, a rainbow will appear. I've come to see that this is God's way of reminding us that He is with us, and under His watch, all things are good."

For an hour it is this kind of talk. I won't bore you with any more details. I tell him a few things about how I feel about losing a friend, but none of them is true. I am not about to bare my soul to a man of the cloth, because that would make me as big a hypocrite as he is.

When my mother left us, my father sat me down and told me that I didn't have to go to church anymore. He wasn't going to force me, he said, because religion was a human invention. "Back when civilization was more primitive, when people possessed no scientific understanding of the world, they needed an explanation for why crops were destroyed by blights, why bad things happened to good people, what happened to them when they died. Death was much more a part of life than it is now; it was expected, even for young people, even for children—lots of disease, and no medicine, of course. Do you understand?"

Then he told me that my mother left because she was sad inside herself and that neither I nor he, outside forces, had anything to do with her sadness, that she had it before she knew us, and that if she chose to believe that God would take care of her, that was fine, but she would have to get medical help to get unsad.

I was only five years old, but I understood that my father was a college professor and that college professors had explanations for everything. Because they were more educated, they did not need religion to make sense of the world.

I do not tell Reverend Black that I'm not about to start believing in God just because Thomas Broughton died.

No one notices me here. I look studious in my carrel. No one knows I'm not always doing my homework; no one knows I'm writing this book, or whatever it is I'm writing. Nobody will find me here.

Do you have any idea how hard a story is to write? My brain is jumpy, and my heart doesn't know where to live. Is Male is such an imperfect narrator, but he will try to finish his tale.

13. Thomas takes another chug of vodka.

(repetition, an effective narrative device)

14. Clay says to Thomas, "Take off your shorts. Take off your boxers."

15. "No way," slurs Thomas. "Not in front of a faggot."

16. Clay goes ape-shit. He lunges at Thomas, but Glenn chases him down and tackles him. They roll around, Clay trying to pin Glenn, Glenn trying to pin Clay, until Clay staggers to his feet and shouts at Thomas, "I am going to kill you! When you get back to dorm, you are as good as dead!" I am not kidding. Those were his exact words, and, unlike Thomas's, they were clear as a bell.

17. Clay thrashes off through the woods with his bottle of vodka.

18. I look at Thomas, who is drunk and laughing his head off.

Ah! how cheerfully we consign ourselves to perdition!

THURSDAY, OCTOBER 12, 9:15 P.M.

Wearing Down Seven Number-Two Pencils

Here in the library among the Great American Poets, most of whom are dead, I am using up lots of paper because of the rock. I need an editor. Scissors cut paper. Who am I to be writing a book? To quote Emily Dickinson, "I am Nobody," but of course she was talking about God, not me.

And she may have a point there, I decide this morning. I push my chair back from the carrel. There has to be a photograph of Emily somewhere around here. I am lost in the smell of old books, I am lost trying to remember what day it is, and I am lost because I can't find her photograph anywhere. I look at my watch. Almost time for class. I look at my syllabus for English. Miss Dovecott must really like Emily, because we only spent a couple of days on Walt. She should never have told us he was gay; we tuned out after that.

41

When I turn back to my carrel to pack up my things, Miss Dovecott is suddenly there. She is there and smiling at me. "You beat me to the punch," she says, leaning over the partition.

"What punch?" I say, slamming this journal shut, thinking, God, I wish there were punch, I wish it were spiked, I wish that Miss Dovecott would drink a gallon of it and make crazy love to me.

"Emily Dickinson. I came to see if I could find the daguerreotype of her."

Daguerreotype?

She is reading my mind, one I am trying to keep clean.

"It's what they used before modern photography," she tells me.

"I didn't know that," I say.

She is looking up at me. She has to. I am taller than she is. In class, she is taller than we are because we are always sitting. Now I am a giant. Fee, fi, fo, fum.

"I liked your essay," she says. I am going, going deep, going into the deep of her brown eyes.

" 'What I Carry,' " she prompts.

"Oh. Oh," I say. I am a scintillating conversationalist.

"I'll give it back in class today. I think you'll be pleased."

"Yes, ma'am," I say. Pleased, pleasing, pleasure. Pleasure me, Miss Dovecott. As she reaches up for the book, the one she is looking for, her sweater rises, and I see the skin of her lower back. I think about that skin all morning long and all through cross-country practice this afternoon while I'm running the trail. Ladies and gentlemen, it keeps me pumping for a good long while.

42

Green Fields

I heard about her before I ever saw her. A young female teacher, good-looking (as in, if she passed you on the street, you would turn your head to check her out), had come to Birch to teach fifth-form English. The minute my dad and I showed up for the start of my junior year and began moving my stuff into 313 Wimberley Hall, Joe Bonnin rushed in to tell me, trying to tone it down because my dad was with me, but I got the message: my new English teacher was a fox.

So let me use this page to record my first moments with Miss Dovecott, because if we become one of the great love stories of all time, these first moments should go on record, should they not?

I was seated with my eleven classmates (now ten) in the classroom. Through the panes of glass in the tall windows, morning light rained and ricocheted across our desks, our arms, our heads. The wooden door skidded along the floor, and her right foot entered in its tasseled brown loafer, the leg bare almost up to the knee. Then the left foot, and then she was standing before the big desk she claimed by setting books on top of it, books that slid away from each other. She looked up and faced us head-on, her gaze sweeping across us like wind over a field. She opened the middle drawer of her desk and drew out a sheet of paper, and in a low, calm voice, she read out our names. By the time she came to mine, I was quivering.

What I Carry

I am quivering, too, when she hands back the essay. She has given me an A-. Or, as she would put it, I have *earned* an A-. I dash back to my room after class, forgetting about my other life for a minute until I open the door and see that Clay's bed has been removed by housekeeping. He has left me with Christie Brinkley and Cheryl Tiegs in their bathing suits, posters I take down, roll into thin tubes, and store in his empty closet. Except for the residue of tape on the walls, there is no trace of him visible, because this is my room now: lucky 313. So much space all to myself, but who is that? I am holding fast to the doorknob when Glenn enters without knocking and pushes me over.

"Stromm," he says, reading my face, "what's wrong?"

I tell him I might have written more than I should have and that Miss Dovecott invited me in to talk about what happened that day at the river. Big mistake. BIG MISTAKE.

"Give me the essay," he says, stretching out his hand. "Give me it."

"I don't have it."

"Bullshit." Glenn lunges for my book bag.

"You can look for it all you want," I say, "but it's not there."

"Then, where it is?"

"She kept it," I lie. It's folded in half inside my journal/ novel/whatever. My journal/novel/whatever is on the shelf in the library behind the giant volume of *Moby-Dick,* where it will stay. I do not dare, do not dare, carry it to dorm.

"You have to go back," Glenn is saying. "You have to go

talk to her; otherwise, you look like you have something to hide."

"Right," I say.

What Miss Dovecott Wrote

(I like it so much that I am copying it here.)

> *Alex—You have courage, and your honesty compels you to hunt down the right phrasing. I admire that. Should you choose to rewrite this one, try to begin fewer sentences with* I. *Try to stand outside and look in, which will allow you more perspective.—Ms. D.*
>
> *P.S. Should you want to talk about that day at the river, I am here for you. I am worried about you. Please come see me.*

I find it intimate, to be addressed by name; I find it thrilling, my name in her handwriting. A woman's handwriting. Male teachers do not write personal notes on our work. They do not use words like "courage" in their comments.

202 Sellers Hall

So after cross-country practice, I do what Glenn says (Ah! how cheerfully we consign ourselves to perdition!), but she is not there. On the walls of her classroom: quotations, quotations, quotations, copied in her neat, elegant handwriting, black marker on construction paper, all different colors.

"Wearing down seven number-two pencils is a good day's work."—Ernest Hemingway

45

"Poetry is all metaphor."—Robert Frost

"If I feel physically as if the top of my head were taken off, I know that is poetry."—Emily Dickinson

"The title is the writer's stamp of approval."—Anonymous

"It is better to fail in originality than to succeed in imitation."—Herman Melville. F^ck you, Her-man. (Is Male must censor his book because it is shelved in a school library.)

On her shelves: dictionaries, thesauri (is that a word?), grammar handbooks, short story anthologies, poetry collections, every Great American Novel known to man (and woman). A framed certificate inscribed to Haley Avis Dovecott, recipient of the F. Scott Fitzgerald English Award, Princeton University, May 1982.

On her desk: a photograph of a man and woman (her parents?) standing in front of a barn; a carved wooden box (inside, rubber bands and paper clips); stacks of homework to grade; her notes for English 500.

Her notes for English 500. My name in the top-right corner: *Alex.* The x trails down, begins the circle that loops around my name. My name is a bull's-eye. X marks the spot.

Hide-and-Seek

I smell her all over the classroom, she smells like baby powder. I leave her a note, her name on top, mine on the bottom, to let her know I have reported in as she oh-so-subtly suggested I do.

Miss Dovecott strikes me as the type who could never have enough fresh flowers in her house. If I brought her flowers—which I will not do, don't worry—she would probably remember them for the rest of her life. I believe that I

46

will publish a poem one day in Miss Dovecott's secret voice, her non-lilting, non-teaching voice. It might go like this:

I nip them at night from the bed
outside the dining hall—daffodils,
hyacinths. In the morning I cradle
them to class in a vase. My students
ask where I got them, they know
I don't have a yard of my own.
I say I got them from the place
inside me that has to bloom
then die to make room for more green.
They call me a thief, but they smile.

—Alex Stromm (1966–)

Gingerbread Night

Suddenly, like daffodils in spring, Miss Dovecott is everywhere in my life. Including at seated dinner, a boarding school staple: Monday, Tuesday, Wednesday, Thursday, Sunday. We make polite conversation regarding stuff no one cares anything about. Birch students take turns being waiters, and whether you are waiting or eating (waiters eat last, after everyone else), you rotate to a new table each week. Sometimes you get a good table, but sometimes you get stuck. There's a faculty member at each table, and the object is to sit as far away from them as possible. The faculty member serves the meat, and then you pass around the side dishes. I never eat the cooked carrots or the steamed broccoli, which have all of the color sucked right out of them. There is always dessert.

47

This week, I am assigned to Mr. McGreavey's table, but Mr. McGreavey has just been nabbed to drive an injured soccer player to the hospital in Asheville, so Miss Dovecott is filling in for him because new teachers share tables with the veterans. (She usually sits with Mr. Henley, the head of her department.) For once, guys are scrambling to sit next to the teacher, but the only seat left when I arrive is three seats down from her on the same side of the table. Miss Dovecott is doing her duty to initiate interesting dinnertime conversation, but her voice is low, and I can't hear what she's saying.

All conversation stops when the waiter serves the dessert, and Ted Ferenhardt, a senior, starts up with the noises. He pours thick white sauce over the square of gingerbread; we watch the liquid slink from its silver pitcher. Miss Dovecott's face goes to stone as Ted moans softly, once. Nathan Brummels, a buddy of Ted's, picks up where Ted leaves off and moans again. Then back to Ted, who adds facial expressions. Moan, moan. Then Nathan. They are quiet about it, but make no mistake, they are enjoying themselves.

Miss Dovecott rises from her chair. "Stop. Right now." Everyone does. I am looking down at my plate, fumbling with my dessert fork. "That is what's known in the real world as sexual harassment. You could get fired from a job for it. Some of you men—and I use that term ironically—are in for a rude awakening when you leave these hallowed halls." She does not look at anyone when she lowers herself back into her chair and says, with no inflection, "Please pass the sauce."

I want to smile, I want to cheer, not the kind of stupid cheer Ted leads us in at the pep rallies. I want to give her a big pat on the back, but just then a wadded-up napkin hits me in the head. I turn and see Glenn at the next table. He raises his eyebrows, amused; he has seen the whole thing. He is still watching when Miss Dovecott folds her napkin neatly by her plate and excuses herself before the bell has rung to dismiss us. She hurries down the long aisle of the dining hall as six hundred eyes crawl over her like black bugs.

Vermin

Right after dinner, Glenn tracks me down. He finds me standing at the library water fountain. He whispers in my ear to meet him in the bathroom in the basement, so I do. There is one toilet, one sink, and a bolt lock on the door, which he slides shut.

"What's going on, Stromm? What did she say during your little talk?"

"Nothing," I tell him. "We haven't talked yet."

"Bullshit."

"Don't worry. There's nothing she could possibly know because she didn't get there in time to see anything."

"Not unless you told her," says Glenn.

"Now, why would I do that?"

"Because your brains are in your crotch."

"I'm not going to do anything stupid. My dad would kill me for getting kicked out of here."

"Mine, too," he says. "But what if Miss Dovecott got there sooner than we think she did? What if she was spying on us the whole time?"

"Then she would have said. We'd have been kicked out by now if she'd gotten there earlier. Don't you think?"

"Yeah, but there's something about her I don't trust. Mark

49

my words: she'll turn Ferenhardt and Brummels in for what they did at dinner."

"I bet you five dollars she won't," I say. "She won that round."

Glenn holds out his hand. "I'll take that bet. You're going to owe me some money when the demerit sheet gets posted tomorrow."

We shake on it. "I've got homework to do," I say, unlocking the door. But inside, my brain is screaming at me, Whatever you tell her, don't mention the vodka, don't bring up Glenn's name. Because whatever happens, Glenn won't rat me out, just as I won't rat him out. It's hard to explain to someone who doesn't live here day in and day out, but the situation with Clay was different. Glenn and I are friends, and you don't tell on friends. It is the real Birch code of honor, the one the students truly embrace, and we will follow it to the end.

Not ignoring what is good, I am quick to perceive a horror.

SATURDAY, OCTOBER 14, 1:20 P.M.

Me too, *Her*-man. Horror is everywhere. It's not like I can run away, unless I want to hitchhike or climb a few mountains like the Trapp Family Singers. After Thomas dies, the only way I can escape is by doing my homework, every last bit of it. Who knew I could be such an excellent student? Now I dot every "i," cross every "t." My teachers applaud my attention to detail. And voila, I am in the spotlight.

Rock, Paper, Scissors

19. Thomas is drunk, way more drunk than Glenn and I.

20. We take off our shoes (but leave our shorts and boxers on).

21. We climb onto the rock. Glenn and Thomas have grown up pulling stunts like this. Being a cautious only child, I just pretend that I have. There are no guys from my hometown around to call my bluff.

22. Glenn jumps.
23. Thomas and I do Rock, Paper, Scissors.
24. Thomas dives.
25. Before I even realize it, I jump, too.

As If the Top of My Head Were Taken Off

Miss Dovecott tells us that Emily Dickinson posed for the daguerreotype when she was seventeen. She passes it around the classroom Friday morning and asks us to stare into Emily Dickinson's eyes. When it gets to Auggie van Dorn, he starts giggling. Emily is homely. She has fat lips, a bunch of moles, and hair that looks oiled to her head. She is seriously unattractive.

Except for the eyes. They are black, they are deep, they know all.

After the Walt Whitman failure, Miss Dovecott knows we will protest Emily Dickinson and her poems. We will say she is a crazy woman who never leaves her attic; we will say she aches for the Grim Reaper to sneak into her bed at night and ravish her. Miss Dovecott knows she is going to have to wow us to get us to like anything at all about Emily.

"So much of Dickinson," she tells us, "is about what is left unsaid and what is left unclear. What we aren't able to articulate, what we aren't able to find the words for—that's what underscores these poems and what, as Dickinson so aptly perceived, lies beneath all of our experiences."

Uh-huh. We nod.

"Because Dickinson's poems were written in the form of hymns," Miss Dovecott explains, mapping out iambic tetrameter and iambic trimeter on the blackboard, "we can sing

52

them, and as we sing them, we can hear where the rhythm slips, where Dickinson disregards, maybe even snubs, that sacred form." So many eyes glazed over; Glenn Everson, dutifully taking notes or plotting a murder—it's hard to tell. "What else might she be snubbing?"

No one answers, no one is going to answer. She repeats the question. No hands go up. So Miss Dovecott starts singing poem #389—"There's been a Death, in the Opposite House"—to the tune of the *Gilligan's Island* theme song.

By the time she reaches the fourth stanza, we are laughing.

The Minister—goes stiffly in—
As if the House were His—
And He owned all the Mourners—now—
And little Boys—besides—

We are laughing at the minister's stiff entry; we are laughing at Miss Dovecott because she can't sing. Suddenly our teacher seems like the weird girl in junior high who wore granny dresses.

At the board, she points to what is written there. "So iambic tetrameter alternating with iambic trimeter is a common form in all types of songs." She puts her hands on the back of her chair. "Now. Even though the death happened in the 'opposite house,' it still affects the speaker. How?"

Andy Hedron raises his hand. "She sees the aftermath of it."

"Right, Andy, but why do you think the speaker is female?"

Auggie jumps in. "Because Emily is a woman. Although she kinda looks like a man."

We laugh, but Miss Dovecott ignores us. "Can you find any evidence in the poem itself that the speaker is female?" The room is so silent that I can hear the fluorescent lights overhead. A couple of guys are gazing out the window. "Okay. Everybody. Look at the poem. It's there. See if you can find it."

"What are we looking for again?" asks Jovan Davis.

"Is it in the third paragraph?" asks Malcolm Marshall.

"Third *stanza*, Malcolm."

I look at the third stanza, singing it to the *Gilligan's Island* theme in my head:

> *Somebody flings a Mattress out—*
> *The Children hurry by—*
> *They wonder if it died—on that—*
> *I used to—when a Boy—*

I don't get it, so I study my corduroy knees.

"What is that last line saying there? Can you put it in your own words?"

Colin Bates (nickname: Master) raises his hand. " 'I used to when *I was* a boy'?"

"Good. Used to what?"

"Used to imagine that the mattresses thrown out of windows were deathbeds," Glenn says. I jerk my head to look at him. He is giving her his cool eyes.

"Well done, Glenn," she says.

"I don't think the speaker is a boy," says Malcolm. "I think he's a man. Because of 'used to,' like he no longer is a boy."

"Now we're getting somewhere."

"I was wondering about this," Auggie says. "I think the Minister is God. The way she capitalizes *His*."

"The house is the church," says Master.

"The house can't be a church," says Jovan. "The house is a house, man."

Suddenly I get it, I get it. I raise my hand. She calls on me. "In the boy's eyes, the minister is like God. When he was a boy, not a man. So it's like when the minister enters the house, the house becomes a church, you know, God's house."

"Good, Alex," Miss Dovecott says, clapping. "Very good. Keep going. So what, according to this poem, does this minister-God own?"

"All the mourners," I say. "And little boys. Dickinson is saying he owns all of us."

She claps again—we are in the swing of it now—and then Glenn says slowly, with eyes as pale as water, "God does not own you, Stromm. God does not own any of us."

Miss Dovecott stares back at him, but his gaze does not waver. "Let's back up now," she says, "and talk about that window." But she can't get us to do it, to explain why it opened like a pod, abruptly, mechanically. The mighty Achilles has silenced us, and Miss Dovecott has to stand there and watch her students fold into themselves, hunching away from the window in the poem, from the windows in the classroom, from everything. One of these students, the one who lost five dollars for believing in the woman he loves, wants desperately to come back to her world—her heavenly wide-open world—but it is roped off now, like an unsafe balcony.

Our World

Ten p.m. Friday night (last night). Outside the freshman dorm, upperclassmen in masks and no shirts stomp in unison. "New boys! New boys!" they chant, shaking their lit torches. Two years ago, at my first pep rally, I was afraid to come out of my dorm.

"Here they come!" someone shouts, and torches flare as the third-formers creep out the front door. Their hands fly to their foreheads, shielding their eyes, as they get absorbed by the mob. The crowd lurches across the quad, down the hill, and into the end zone of the football field. The cheer masters leap onto the wooden platform built especially for these occasions. When they raise their torches, the muscles in their biceps and shoulders harden.

"Are you ready?" the head cheer master, Ted Ferenhardt, shouts. Tonight he is a giant in an Afro wig, cutoff jean shorts, and combat boots. His chest is slick with Vaseline. The crowd roars back. "Are you ready?"

On the sidelines, a flock of frightened faculty children take a few steps back into the shadows where their parents are huddled.

"Chase Harper!" the cheer masters yell and clap in rhythm. "Chase Harper!" The quarterback of the football team hops onto the platform. One of the cheer masters hands him a torch.

"New boys!" shouts Chase. "You see this torch? This is what you are going to have to be for us tomorrow. Every single one of you better be in those stands cheering your guts

56

out. If you don't, you run the gauntlet, and you all know what that means. Now, let's hear it! Go, Bulldogs! Go, Bulldogs!"

All of the new boys are yelling it now. "Go, Bulldogs!" The defensive line of the football team mobs the stage: more guys with painted chests, more guys with wigs and masks. Out of the mass rises a new chant, a slower one that folds on itself one screeching letter at a time: "B! U! L! L! D! O! G! S! Gooooooo, Dawgs! Dawgs! Dawgs! Dawgs!" The guys on the stage erupt into chaotic barking, and Ted silences them by raising his torch.

"Who's ready to kiss the Buddha?" he shouts. Chip Donnelly, with his jiggling stomach, struggles onto the platform, and Ted puts his hand on the other boy's shoulder. The two of them scan the crowd with demonic eyes. "Where is he?" Ted shouts. "Where's the Little Dipper?"

The Little Dipper is the younger brother of the Big Dipper, who got caught dipping tobacco during the first week of his new-boy year and racked up sixty demerits, which took five months to work off. Eyes wide, Lane Carter raises his hand, shaking, and he climbs onto the stage. His big brother, Silas, a cheer master, stands at the back of the stage, laughing his head off while the Little Dipper drops to his knees in front of Chip's sumo wrestler stomach.

"Kiss the Buddha!" the crowd is shouting. "Kiss the Buddha!" The Little Dipper bows his head and puts his hands over his mouth, and Ted jumps behind him, arms spread and flapping like wings. He screams into the back of Lane Carter's head, "Kiss the Buddha!" When Lane looks up, there are tears on his cheeks, and the Buddha grabs Lane's head and pushes it into his stomach. The cheer masters hop up and down, and the crowd roars.

Not ignoring what is good, I am quick to perceive a horror. One of the little kids standing next to Miss Dovecott runs back to his father, a chemistry teacher, and lifts his arms to the sky, begging to be picked up. Miss Dovecott crosses her arms and hugs herself.

Green Fields

My new-boy year, to avoid the second pep rally because the first one was so scary, I snuck out of study hall one Friday night ten minutes before the bell rang and hid in the chapel until I knew it was over. I sat in the back of the room in study hall. Mr. Lyme, the proctor, could hardly see his own wristwatch, not to mention what was happening where I was. I slid to the floor and crawled out. No one ratted on me. Other guys in study hall saw me do it and laughed, but they never turned me in, and Mr. Lyme, who was ancient, didn't hear them, just as he didn't hear me zip up my backpack and drop to the floor like I was escaping from an ambush. Which, of course, I was.

Our World, the Sequel

Last year, I played Would You Rather all the time on dorm. Now that Miss Dovecott has become a piece on the game board, it is much less funny.

Basically, the game goes like this: you sit around in someone's room with the door closed and offer up a scenario involving Birch School characters and/or movie stars. Sex is almost always involved.

For example, Would you rather watch Mrs. Davido give a blow job to the Buddha or Mr. Lyme? The best answer in this case is "Neither," but in the world of Would You Rather, that is not an option.

I am with Joe Bonnin and Andy Hedron after the pep rally, before Lights-Out, when I have to be back in my room. Their room is so different from most guys' rooms. That is to say, it is not wallpapered with posters of *Sports Illustrated* swimsuit models. Joe owns one poster of Brooke Shields in her Calvins and two of the UNC basketball team, and Andy has got to be the only guy on campus with a poster of Audrey Hepburn à la *Breakfast at Tiffany's*—very understated foxy.

"Would You Rather?" Joe says.

"Here we go," says Andy.

"Would you rather watch Miss Dovecott give a blow job to Gaybrook or Everson?"

"Who cares about Gaybrook?" I say. "He's gone."

"Gaybrook," says Andy. "No way she could get him off. Hey, but I bet Everson could."

"Gaybrook," I say, and nod.

"I'm going with Everson," says Joe. "He'd splooge in about two seconds."

"So would you," Andy says.

"Yeah, I know, but it'd be interesting because Everson can't stand her."

"What do you mean?" I ask, but I know exactly what he means.

"He's the only one in this whole school who doesn't want to do her."

"Maybe he just doesn't like English," I say.

59

"She's cool," said Andy. "I'd definitely do her."

"Me too," I say, but it's not exactly what I mean. What I mean is, I would like to lie on a bed with her, her face an inch from mine.

"Hey," says Andy, "would you rather watch Mr. Olson or Reverend Black roasted alive over a slow-burning fire?"

"Black," Joe and I say in unison.

"Juicier," adds Joe.

"Ballpark franks," says Andy. "Plump when you cook 'em."

Hide-and-Seek

Miss Dovecott finds me this morning at breakfast. I am sitting by myself at the head of a long table, cramming for my Latin test.

"I've been looking for you," she says.

I smile a closed-mouth smile to keep scrambled eggs from falling out.

"Do you have a minute?"

I nod.

"Finish your breakfast," she says. "I'll be in my classroom."

But when I get to her classroom, Mr. Henley, the head of the English department, is there. They are looking at a sheet of paper that Miss Dovecott is holding in her hand. When I knock, they look up like they're accusing me of something. Miss Dovecott comes to the door.

"Alex," she says, "we'll have to talk later. But now that you're here"—she holds up the paper in her hand, a photograph torn from a magazine—"do you happen to know anything about this?"

I shake my head and say, "No." Because I don't.

60

Better to Fail in Originality than Succeed in Imitation

In class, Miss Dovecott holds it up to show us all. She explains that someone left the photograph of the naked woman on her desk. Across the glossy breasts, someone has drawn a picture of a very large penis with a typed caption: "Miss Dovecott and Moby's Dick."

Everyone knows it's her favorite novel; she talks about it all the time, saying how we should read it on our own, which of course none of us will. Miss Dovecott makes sure we have a very good look at the artwork before she sets it facedown on her desk. No one has confessed thus far, she says. She wants to know if we know anything about it. It's embarrassing—we are embarrassed for her—and we look away. Truth be told, the picture could have been torn out of any of the hundreds of porn magazines stuffed under mattresses or stashed behind toilets all over campus. I glance at Glenn; he is staring straight ahead at nothing. He looks the way he looked when we gathered in the hall of our dorm last year and listened to Spalding Frazier break up with his girlfriend over the phone. I remembered thinking that Glenn, who also had a girlfriend at the time, would have handled a breakup differently: using the pay phone in the gym or writing the girl a letter. He would never have done it in public.

All during English class, Miss Dovecott keeps her arms folded across the front of her white turtleneck sweater. I remember the first day she wore this sweater: September 22. (Is that the first official day of autumn? I can never get those equinoxes straight.) I wrote it in my notes for that day—"sweater"—which was a reminder for me down the road

61

that I didn't pay one bit of attention in class to what I was supposed to be paying attention to. The sweater makes her breasts look big. Today she looks the way I feel—which is to say that sometimes, I don't know what to do or how to feel.

I love to sail forbidden seas, and land on barbarous coasts.

The Samuel E. Walter IV Memorial Library is my rock. My Rock of Gibraltar. If I go back to dorm with this book in my hands, there is nowhere I can hide it, nowhere where it won't be found. I will be cut, cut to shreds, if anyone, especially Glenn, finds this. This is the hard part to put on paper.

Rock, Paper, Scissors

Glenn tells Thomas to watch closely, to jump and not dive, to be sure that he knows exactly how far he needs to sling his body to clear the shallows.

After he comes up sputtering for air, Glenn yells up to us, "Double jump! I dare you!" I turn to Thomas, he turns to me. I am about to say, Maybe we shouldn't, and then Glenn shouts again from the water.

So I go, "Rock, Paper, Scissors"—the last words I ever speak to Thomas—and one, two, three, he holds out rock, I hold out paper. Thomas dives through the sky. I do not wait for him to surface before I jump.

The sick thing is that after I go under, I pretend like I'm drowning. I pop up, flailing my arms, opening my mouth wide, making gasping noises. I'm not even looking at Thomas—or for him. I'm flopping around in the water. Over my own fake drama, I hear Glenn scream Thomas's name.

Right before Thomas dove, he said things.

25. Before I even realize it, I jump, too. We all go into the river. See Dick and Jane go under. Jump, Dick. Jump, Jane. (If only I were writing a children's book. If I were writing a children's book, I'd be done by now.) But Thomas does not jump, he dives. Thomas enters the water headfirst.

26. Thomas's head finds a rock that is harder than his head.

27. His lungs fill with water.

28. Drown, Thomas, drown.

A Rough Draft

October 15, 1982

Dear Mr. and Mrs. Broughton,

I have been wanting to write for a couple of weeks now, but I did not know exactly what to say or how to say it, so I have put it off. Now I realize that I will never know exactly what to say or how to say it.

I am profoundly sorry for the loss of your son. He was a good friend to me, and I mean that. I wish I could have been the person who saved Thomas's life that day, rather than a person who was with him when he died. It all happened so fast. I guess you know that the rock is now off-limits, and that is good because it is dangerous and we never should have jumped from it.

People like to say that boys will be boys. But I have never liked that expression, because it sounds like an excuse. I have no excuse to offer you, just my heartfelt apology and my sympathy.

Most sincerely,
Alexander Stromm

P.S. Please extend my sympathies to Trenton.

SUNDAY, OCTOBER 15, 8:48 P.M.

Green Fields

And Thomas was a good friend. The fact that he was an uncomplicated guy made him that way. You could argue with Thomas over the littlest stuff, and even if it snowballed into a fight, he wouldn't hold it against you. Like a lot of people, he liked arguing for the sake of arguing. His father was a hotshot litigator, so he came by it honestly.

Like I wrote in the essay, Thomas and I really did go down to the river to fish sometimes, and although we talked about doing it, we never brought along anything illegal (i.e., pot) when it was just the two of us. We played by the rules, and that was nice because we didn't have to worry about Dean Mansfield jumping out of the bushes during one of his "nature walks," as he calls them, although we call them "patrol strolls." Thomas would pack us a lunch (peanut butter crackers, Snickers bars, a couple of apples), and I would take care of the bait. We didn't fly-fish—too many trees—so I dug up worms and grubs in the early morning after a rain. Although I never told Thomas this, I felt like we were Huck Finn and Tom Sawyer before Injun Joe entered the picture.

As far as Great American Novels go, put me down for *Huckleberry Finn*. It's a hell of a lot better than *Moby-Dick*; I am having a hard time getting past the first chapter of that one. I read the library's copy sometimes when I get writer's block. Miss Dovecott says that schools don't teach it anymore because there isn't time enough during the academic year to cover all of the Greats. It makes her sad that such a fine novel collects dust on a shelf. It's good for me, though, because a big book gives me something to hide behind.

Green Fields Gone

This afternoon in my room that I used to share with Clay, I copy the letter onto stationery with my name across the top, but what if it makes Mrs. Broughton cry? What if she and Mr. Broughton already hate me forever? I had not had the guts to offer them my condolences in person, and as soon as I drop the letter through the mail slot, I regret it.

The Artists

As I'm walking back from the post office, Miss Dovecott catches up with me. "Maybe you have a minute or two," she says, pointing to a bench in the quadrangle. Another cold, hard bench. I feel sick to my stomach.

"I'll get straight to the point," she says. The point is that she finds my writing exciting. My most recent essay revealed to her that of all the students she teaches, I am the most observant. I have the sensitivity of a person twice my age. She believes that I feel things with my heart that I'm unable to put into words. She calls me a natural-born poet. As she says all of these things that no one has ever said to me before, she follows my eyes with hers, which are dark and deep like pockets.

"You are on my side," she says.

"What side is that?" I ask.

"The winning side," she says, and smiles. "The team of artists."

"Who are we playing?"

"The barbarians," she says. "We are always playing them."

The Barbarians

Glenn is waiting for me—in my room—when I return from the quadrangle. He is sitting at my desk, and the middle drawer is open.

"You are brilliant," he whispers.

"What do you mean?"

"The giant penis on Dovecott's desk."

"I didn't put it there."

"Like hell you didn't," Glenn says.

"I think *you* did. And I bet Miss Dovecott thinks so, too."

"Why the hell would she think that?"

"Because you did," I say.

"So maybe I did. It's part of The Plan."

"What plan?"

"The one to figure out how much she knows."

"Glenn, we have to be careful. There doesn't have to be a *plan*. It's way too dangerous and completely unnecessary."

"She knows, Stromm. She knows something, and she's not telling us or Dean Mansfield or Mr. Armstrong. She's

67

keeping it all to herself, and you are the perfect one to find out what it is."

"Why were you looking through my desk?" I ask.

"Pencil," he says, raising one up in the air, and he writes out The Plan, with a line for signatures beneath it. Is Male signs it. Because he loves to sail forbidden seas, and land on barbarous coasts.

The Plan

1. Mess with Miss Dovecott psychologically (as in the photo/drawing left on her desk).

2. Act innocent. Do all the homework; answer promptly and intelligently during class.

3. Make sure she is at the final pep rally.

4. Glenn: Tell Dean Mansfield she makes you uncomfortable when you go in for one-on-one help. Glenn: Go in for one-on-one help.

5. Alex: Use your writing to lure her. (This step is my contribution, though I do not tell Glenn what Miss Dovecott said to me in the quad.)

6. If she knows more than she's telling, move in for the kill.

Glenn Albright Everson, III, Class of 1984

Achilles in the flesh. If you were a casting agent and were looking for someone to play the legendary Greek hero, Glenn would be your man. Two years ago, I wanted to be Glenn. I wanted his blond curly hair; I wanted his brain. I wanted his walk, his athleticism, his easy way with other guys. It wasn't lust. I wanted his house on the golf course, his happy-looking family, his girlfriend with the thick brown hair. I wanted his whole entire history.

Our first year at Birch, he invited me to his house for Thanksgiving. He had overheard me say that I was supposed to spend it with my mom and didn't want to. So I told my mom that she and Victor could go on to Aspen without me (which I knew they wanted to do anyway), and I rode down to Charlotte with Glenn on the bus. The room I stayed in had a fireplace. Glenn let his dog, Bailey, an old black lab, sleep with me because he knew I missed my own dog. At Thanksgiving dinner, Mrs. Everson poured me a small glass of wine, and when I drank that, she poured me a second one, no questions asked. The Eversons ate by candlelight, even though it was only four o'clock. Afterward, everyone gathered in the living room, and we had to say one thing we were thankful for. I said I was thankful to have a friend like Glenn. Then they told family stories, and I listened and laughed. Glenn's big sister, a junior in college, told me that I was an old soul. She said I had a great smile. That night, Glenn's dad lit the logs in the fireplace in my room, and I slept like a baby, Bailey at my feet. In the morning, when I woke, I hugged Bailey to me as I watched the last orange ember burn itself out.

For the rest of the school year, Glenn and I played cards together on dorm and tossed the football around outside in the quad. Glenn showed me that I had interesting things to say because he encouraged me to say them; all the other guys I knew would rather hear themselves talk. One day Glenn asked me what I thought happened when we die, and I told him, "Nothing. We rot in the earth." I told him that the idea of coming from dust and returning to dust was the one believable thing in the Bible, and he looked at me, wide-eyed, like I was some kind of prophet.

But he was the teacher, not me. When the weather grew warmer, he taught me the basics of lacrosse, a game I had barely even heard of before I came to Birch, but I wasn't very coordinated and got cut from the first round of the freshman team tryouts. He was the only freshman who made the varsity squad, and I couldn't help but wonder, out of all the guys in the class, why Glenn had chosen me.

And then, at the end of our sophomore year, Glenn didn't ask me to be his roommate, and he turned into someone I didn't know as well as I thought I did. I honestly believe that if Glenn hadn't roomed with Thomas, Thomas would still be alive.

Is Male, No Middle Name, No Roman Numerals, Class of 1984

Once a blank slate; now an above-average student from a broken family. Lives with father, son of German immigrants, in a town you've never heard of (Black Mountain) in an A-frame house hidden from the road. Will attend a state-supported university (but probably not the one where his father teaches) and will be considered a man of mystery by the coeds because of his seldom-seen dimple. Will go down in the record books as agreeing to The Plan because friendship is more important than romance. Will go down in the record books as being responsible for his friend Thomas Broughton's death. Is Male could have saved Thomas, maybe, if Is Male hadn't been goofing around in the water. Is Male had worked as a lifeguard the summer before at a camp, where he'd earned extra

70

money by cleaning the mess hall and the bathrooms. Is Male was a janitor.

MONDAY, OCTOBER 16, 7:13 A.M.

Poetry Is All Metaphor

Thomas doesn't come to me in dreams. He comes to me just before that, when I'm trying to sleep. I write poems when I can't sleep. I write them in my head and memorize them for the morning, when I can record them in the light of day.

When I was in the third form, a starling got caught in some electrical wire hanging from the high ceiling of our dorm's porch. Thomas stood there with me, watching it. Helpless together, we were near tears because the bird was going to tear its wing off trying to escape, and we decided the humane thing to do was to put it out of its misery. The whole incident has been burning inside me for almost two years, so I figure I might as well write a poem about it. Here it is.

On his way to class, the boy hears the wild beat of wings.
Others hear, too; they gather on the porch, heads jerked back.
Near the top of a column, in a web of electrical wire,
a sparrow, dull-eyed, hangs by its leg.

(Starlings are birds that push native birds out of their nests; in other words, they're not the nicest birds in the world. So I changed it to a sparrow.)

The boys determine it's been there a day.
David says it looks embarrassed; Sammy asks if he can shoot it.
Russell thinks it will chew its leg off and escape.

71

(Made-up names to protect the innocent)

Scooping a baseball from his backpack, the poet-boy cocks his
    arm.
Last week he wrote a poem about a bird he could not save,
a parakeet named Chuck that died in the cup of his hand
while he yelled to the sky, over and over, "Breathe!"

(In case you were wondering, I never owned a parakeet—
more poetic license.)

Now the boy rips the air, cracking
plaster one inch from the sparrow's head.
He tries again; the ball hits brick, drops to brown leaves.
The third time, he blows on it for luck,
but it loops into an overgrown hedge.
When Russell bails it out and hands it to him,
the poet-boy lingers, half in shadow, half in sun,
squinting like he's saving words for later,
and he lets the ball roll to the ground
like the sound of nothing.

Writing is about making choices, Miss Dovecott says.
One word or phrase or title over another. So many options
that they're almost overwhelming. Which is why it is sometimes so easy to grab the cliché, to reach out to what is famil-
iar. But don't. Because metaphor is all about the comparison
of two unfamiliar, unlike things.

. . . one grand hooded phantom, like a snow hill in the air.

I'm getting the distinct feeling that Moby-Dick is a symbol. If he were just a regular black whale, he wouldn't be. So Melville made him white, like a ghost. White is innocent. A month ago, so was I. Miss Dovecott believes that "loss of innocence" is the "overarching theme of Western literature." Maybe; I haven't read enough of it to say. But her definition is deficient. *Loss of innocence* is not the small and/or giant steps that lead to the gray areas, the complexities, that are the substance of adulthood. *Loss of innocence* is the knowledge that your brain, no matter how much you cajole it, can never make your heart pure. My brain has been so unfaithful. It has tricked me into alliances I didn't even know I'd formed.

Lovely in Her Bones

First thing Monday morning (yesterday), Miss Dovecott asks us to get out our syllabi; we are going to make a change because we need more in-depth work with the concept of metaphor.

Syllabi. All of our teachers must have taken Latin. I take Latin, too, but I'm not in the honors section. Does Miss Dovecott have ulterior motives for replacing the innocuous "The Author to Her Book," by Anne Bradstreet—which, for the record, is rife with implied comparison—with "I Knew a Woman," by Theodore Roethke? Glenn is certain that she does, and I have to admit, he might have a point. For homework, we are to track, through all four stanzas, the poem's use of metaphor. It's the dirtiest poem I've read in my entire life.

(X-Rated) Homework

"That woman in the poem must have been hot," Ben Wilson says to me this morning as I sling my backpack onto my desk to retrieve my homework. I look at Miss Dovecott to see if she has heard. She is smiling, pulling at the tip of her ponytail. I would like to take a bath with her and undo that ponytail, see her hair fan out in the water like a mermaid's.

"Teddy Row-Whoever was p-whipped," says Jovan Davis.

"Yep," says Ben.

Joe Bonnin says to Miss Dovecott as we're settling in, "I can't believe that poem was in our book. You finally assigned us something I didn't mind reading."

We are paying attention now, watching to see how she will wade through the sexy imagery in the poem, and I wonder whatever happened with the penis drawing, and though Glenn has refused to own up to it, I am pretty darn sure it was part of The Plan. "Well," she says, "let's first try to sur-mise what Roethke might ultimately be trying to say. If he is speaking to you, what is he telling you? Bailey?"

"Um, maybe he's saying that a woman can change your life."

"Good, good. Change it how?"

More hands go up. She lets Bailey Richards continue. "Maybe change the way you view time?"

"Right. Well done. So, Ben, how does the speaker view time differently?"

"Um, I'm not sure."

"Look at the poem," she says, "and see what you can find. Maybe in the last stanza."

" 'I measure time by how a body sways,' " says Jovan.

"Right, Jovan. So what do you think that's all about?"

"I guess it has something to do with, you know, boom-chicka-boom?"

Most guys are laughing. "Jovan," Miss Dovecott says, "let's try to look beyond that aspect of the poem for just a minute."

"I don't know if I can," says Jovan. "I mean, I'm not try-ing to be a smart-ass, but if it's right there in front of you, you're gonna look at it."

The whole class is laughing now, and when Miss Dove-cott raises her hand to calm us down, we quiet, but our eyes are all over one another's, trying to measure who will pick up where Jovan left off.

"Glenn," she says. "What do you think about the poem's last line?"

"To be honest, I don't think much of it. The poem would have been better without it. I think the line that comes before it is much stronger. Because isn't the message of the poem that he learns from the woman? He *lives* to learn from her, he says. Time has nothing to do with it. He doesn't care about time."

"Yeah, the last line kind of diminishes the rest of the poem, especially with those parentheses," I say, wondering if this is somehow part of The Plan or if Glenn really does believe this.

"Do you think men and women might read this poem differently?" she asks.

Joe Bonnin laughs. "I don't know a single girl who would understand this poem."

"I believe *that*," says Jovan.

Glenn catches my eye before he speaks. "Miss Dovecott, I have to read it like a guy would. There's no other way I can read it."

She does not call on Glenn again even though he is clearly the best reader in the class. When she asks me what I've taken away from the poem, I read aloud from my homework, and I quote: "Roethke is saying that making love to an older woman is as transformative as poetry itself."

I am too embarrassed to look at her, but Glenn tells me later that he watched the blush rise from the triangle of skin beneath her throat.

Elegy for Jane

This afternoon before practice, I look up Roethke poems in the library. There is one I like, "Elegy for Jane." Roethke knew Jane—she was his student—and he wrote a poem for her after she died by being thrown from a horse.

There is nothing sexual about this poem (unfortunately), but there is lots of metaphor: Jane is compared to a fish, a fern, and birds. Maybe she liked nature; maybe, to Roethke, she *was* nature, one grand hooded phantom, like a snow hill in the air. It is a sad and lonely poem, stuck here in this book, which will go back on this shelf when I'm through with it. No one will remember Jane unless they find her poem. Someday, no one will remember me.

Elegy for Poets
by Alex Stromm

We lie on our loamy backs—
quilt-less, quill-less,
no paper, no typewriter—
and forever compare earth
with sky.

One might say we've an endless
supply of material: we have our
night, our grass, our shooting stars,
our dirt and worms, their appetites,
the clouds and all their ways of being
clouds, the roots of trees, the far-off
birds, the sound of air, which is not
the sound of breath.

What verse can prop us up again
on legs of bone and blood and skin?

While I Was Writing My Elegy

This is where I start to doubt my good friend Golden Boy. This is where the ground between us begins to split. According to G.B., this is what supposedly happened.

At nine o'clock p.m., he walked into Miss Dovecott's classroom, where she said she would be between eight and nine. He didn't need help with his homework, a poem to be written in the form and rhyme scheme of Roethke's "My Papa's Waltz," but he pretended to need it.

"She gave me her cool look," Glenn tells me later in my room, "and I gave her mine right back, but she said she'd be glad to help and asked me to tell her how far I'd gotten."

He said to her the same thing I'd been struggling with all evening: "It's hard not to want to use Roethke's words."

"I understand," Miss Dovecott answered. "They stick in your head because of the waltz rhythm."

"Yeah," Glenn agreed, laying a crumpled sheet of notebook paper on her desk. "It's like I'm singing this song in my brain, and I can't get beyond it to find my own song."

"Well, what's your subject?"

"That's the problem. I can't think of anything to write about." Glenn told me that he paused here, his face blank. "Except sex."

From this point on, I am skeptical. As in, I'm not sure how reliable a narrator he is. Glenn says that at first, Miss Dovecott pretended not to hear him, and she placed her shaking hands under her thighs and stared down at her watch for a full minute. But soon enough, words were delivered to

78

Miss Dovecott from somewhere, and she spoke them: "You could write about how you can't find your own song."

"What do you mean?" Glenn asked.

"You just told me that you keep hearing Roethke's words instead of your own. You could write about that, a poem about writer's block. That could be the literal meaning. And then, if you think about it, that literal meaning could also work on a figurative level—how searching for words is comparable to searching for identity."

"Oh." Glenn proceeded slowly. "I thought you meant something else."

According to him, her voice was quick, nervous. "What? What did you think I meant?"

"Never mind," he tossed out.

"No, what? I'm curious." But she wasn't curious, Glenn explains; she was scared.

Which made it the perfect time to execute The Plan. "I thought you were saying that writer's block could be the figurative meaning, and sexual frustration could be the literal."

"You did not say that," I interrupt.

"Hell, yeah, I did."

"What did she do?"

"She asked me to leave."

"Did you?"

"Yeah," he says, "but then I looked at her and said, 'You know how you're always telling us to take whatever in life is confusing us and make a poem out of it to give the confusion some order? Maybe I should make some order out of all this frustration I've been having. Is that what you want me to do?'"

I want to punch him.

Miss Dovecott pushed her chair back. "I just want you to do what you can most easily connect with. What feels most honest, most real." And that was true, I'm sure of it. It was the essential thing—what Miss Dovecott wanted for her students, and for herself. "And I also want you out of here," she said.

"I completely unhinged her. Completely!" Glenn is jubilant.

"Okay, then," I say calmly. "If she's completely unhinged, then we got her. The God-Almighty Stupid Plan is over."

"Oh, no way," says Glenn, grabbing my shoulders and shaking them. "No effing way. We're only halfway there. You are in this, my man." He pulls me to him in a bear hug.

"What are you doing?" I say, pushing him off me. "What the hell are you doing? I've got to get back to work." I gesture to the open books on my desk.

"English?"

"Yep. English." I open the door so that he will leave me alone.

Glenn sashays a few steps to pick up my notebook. "Let me see."

"Put it down," I say.

"No. I want to see what the belle of Birch is writing." But there isn't anything to see—the page is blank—and he throws my notebook at me.

What Thomas Said on the Rock Right Before He Dove: Verbatim

"I saw Clay and Glenn yesterday in the bathroom. They were both coming out of the far left shower at the same time.

Claybrook was sweating like a homo. Is Everson a homo, too?"

What Thomas Really Saw, According to Glenn: Paraphrase

Clay and Glenn in the dorm bathroom, Clay in the left shower, Glenn in the middle one next to it. Glenn had run out of shampoo. He was borrowing Clay's shampoo.

Who ain't a slave? Tell me that.

THURSDAY, OCTOBER 19, 7:12 A.M.

Insomnia, the Sequel

Four a.m. No poems in my head. I want to sneak off dorm with my flashlight, but I'm scared I'll be caught even though no one is awake at this hour and the masters on duty turn in at midnight. Birch doesn't need a security guard. It's already secure: nowhere to run, not a town within miles. Isolation, desolation.

I picture the rock and the night gathered around it. What cliché did Reverend Black use? "Thomas Broughton did not die in vain; he was part of God's plan, a bigger plan than any of us can imagine." Language about death is full of clichés.

Lying there in my bed, I know in my soul of souls that even God does not have the power to intervene in a world where centuries of evil have rooted beneath the surface of everything, a system so complex that no one, not even He, can hack it apart. My father is right: humans made God up to satisfy their own needs.

Trying to Write Poems at 5:00 a.m. but not Getting Past the First Line

> *Guilt hangs from my neck like a piece of rope.*
> *Anger, like teeth pressed in a mouth, cracks its way out.*
> *Sadness is the absence of everything else.*

Rock, Paper, Scissors

While Glenn is giving Thomas CPR on the riverbank, I tell him what Thomas said, what he saw in the bathroom. "Shut up, Stromm," Glenn tells me. But a few minutes later as we are walking up the hill behind Miss Dovecott and the two paramedics, he slips me a stick of gum and glares as he whispers, "Thomas didn't know what he was seeing. Remember that." And so I nod, remembering.

THURSDAY, OCTOBER 19, 5:56 P.M.

Trying to Do My English Homework That I Didn't Do the Night Before

This morning, I am the first person in the library, or so I think. I settle into my carrel and am huddled over a blank sheet of paper when I hear someone, a student's voice I don't recognize, say her name on the other side of the shelves. I sit straight and cold, a column of marble.

"Miss Dovecott was walking down from the top of the hill."

"In the dark?" asks another unfamiliar voice.

"Yeah. It was late."

83

"That's not so weird. English teachers are drawn to the dark side. Or haven't you noticed?"

"Everson said he could see her flashlight from his window."

"But how could he see that far? Wimberley Hall's like a mile away."

"Think about it. The trees are bare now. You can see pretty far when there aren't any leaves, especially from the third floor, and anyway, the flashlight stopped at the infirmary."

"It could have been Nurse Patty."

"Have you seen Nurse Patty ever leave the building? It's like she's glued to it or something."

"Well, that doesn't mean it was Miss Dovecott. It might not have even been a girl."

"It was definitely a girl, Everson said, and she was running. No other girl around here can run that fast."

The breakfast bell rings, and the two guys, whom I still can't place (we all sound alike), rustle into their jackets. I duck behind the carrel, listening to the sound of their boots fade. So Glenn said he saw Miss Dovecott last night walking the trail with a flashlight, and he told some other guy, but why didn't he tell me? My head is like a sewing basket full of needles without a single spool of thread.

THURSDAY, OCTOBER 19, 8:45 P.M.

Homework assignment for October 19, English 500. ("Get out your syllabi; we're making another change," Miss Dovecott announces.)

You are a woman at a yard sale early one Saturday morning. Picture these four items on the sale table: a stuffed monkey, a

84

fishing pole, a dead butterfly in a frame, an empty vodka bottle. "Buy" one of the items and, in this woman's voice (first person), describe where you think the item has been (its past) and where it is going (its future). Describe what attracted you to the item in the first place. Title the piece with the woman's name, first and last. (Two pages handwritten or one page typed.)

What Glenn Whispers to Me on the Way Out of Class

"She knows. Don't choose the bottle."

Scissors, Paper, Rock

The bottle of vodka was empty when Clay left the scene. What if he chucked it into the woods on his way up to campus? Where is that bottle now? I can't believe three weeks have gone by and I haven't thought to ask. Blame it on lack of sleep, which skews things, turns them backward and upside down. Like vodka does.

I wonder now if Thomas had ever had a sip of vodka before September 30. We all act in front of our friends here at Birch like we're these big partyers when we're at home, but I had always believed that Thomas was telling the truth about going through a six-pack of beer without even feeling it. But liquor is different, my dad likes to tell me; once liquor enters a sane person's veins, it can turn him crazy in a way that beer cannot.

After I jump from the rock with all that vodka in my stomach and plunge into the river, I think about what I learned in fourth grade—that 60 percent of me is water.

Running

Miss Dovecott sometimes runs around the track after school. I am walking by this afternoon on my way to practice when I hear Mr. Southey, the JV football coach, whistle at her. She pretends not to hear him, but she hears me when I call out to her. She looks happy to see me and waves and runs for at least fifty meters with a smile on her face.

It might be the running, not the poetry, keeping me sane. I can run the trails now with my eyes closed; I know where the fallen logs are, the exposed roots, the small gullies the rain has created. It has rained for the past two days—a straight, cold rain—but when I'm running, I can actually make myself believe that it's poetic inspiration hitting my head, and it makes me go faster. Mr. Wellfleet doesn't understand why my times are improving, but he is proud of me.

Glenn Albright Everson, III

He is convinced that Miss Dovecott is trying to smoke something out through the English assignment she gave us. He is certain that she is going to analyze our choices to see what it says about us. (He is also certain that Clay was telling the truth when he said he threw the bottle over the barbed-wire fence and into the ravine bordering the Birch School property.)

So Glenn writes about the fishing pole. The woman who buys it, Alice V. Allison, grew up in Maine and went out on the fishing boat with her grandfather when she was a child every single Saturday. Alice imagines that the pole belongs to the husband of the woman selling it, and he doesn't know that she's selling it. He is going to be angry when he finds out, but the seller is tired of the fishing pole hitting her in the head every time she opens the bedroom closet. Alice breaks the pole and gives half to her daughter and half to her son, so that they can pretend they each have a magic wand because they are being brats (as usual) and are embarrassing her here at this yard sale in this very fine neighborhood.

Alexander (No Middle Name) Stromm (No Roman Numerals)

He had a stuffed monkey, still does, on his dresser at home. It was his mother's, and one of the few things he remembers her saying about herself was that she used to dance all over the house with the monkey, up and down the stairs, and out onto the wide green lawn and up and down the sidewalks. She wanted to be Ginger Rogers when she grew up. But Alex's dad wouldn't let him play with the monkey until he was six because he could have pulled off the red ball on the monkey's hat, put it into his mouth, and choked to death. By then, his mother was gone.

Alex writes about the monkey in the voice of Fanny Goole. Fanny is blind. She thinks the monkey is a baby doll because the monkey's tail fell off long ago. She is aware that the doll has very big ears, so, ironically, Fanny Goole names the doll "Bad Monkey" and sleeps with it every night. You think right up until the end of the story that she has bought the doll/monkey for her daughter, but then you find out that it is for Fanny herself. Fanny is kind of retarded.

It is the stupidest thing I have ever written. That's maybe because it is a stupid assignment to begin with. Okay, so I am blaming my shortcomings on the woman I love. I am ashamed of my below-average and unoriginal self.

FRIDAY, OCTOBER 20, 3:00 P.M.

Haley Avis Dovecott, Princeton University, Class of 1982, Magna cum Laude

I stop by her classroom during lunch today and apologize for my lackluster homework. She accepts my apology and tells me she'll give me some extra time to do it over, to get it right. She says she hopes to meet my parents so that she can tell them what a dedicated student I am. I tell her that they aren't able to come to Parents' Weekend this year. Then I ask her about the certificate on the bookshelf, a reading award.

Reading, she tells me, is what she does best. She loves it because it uses the whole of her, the right and the left, the hemispheres of reason and imagination. She discovered as a child that a closed book is a darkness anyone can enter, not a scary darkness like a basement or a storm, but a comforting one that wrapped her up neatly inside a world she could control.

She is talking to me, Miss Dovecott—Haley—is really talking to me. I ache to wrap her in my arms, which she is welcome to control any way she likes. On rare occasions, I have sat in class and envisioned my teachers in their apartments hunched over weak coffee or dazed like zombies standing at their closets, wishing for different lives. But Miss Dovecott doesn't wish for a different life, she wishes to be with me right now, right here, telling me things.

She surprises me with a question: "How does reading make you feel?"

"I've never thought much about it," I answer.

"Okay, then how does math make you feel?"

"Like I don't know anything. Like a loser."

"Now answer the question about reading," she says.

"I guess reading makes me more interested in things—in the world, I mean. It makes me want to know more about people and how they think and what they have done with their lives."

"Me too," she says.

"Math doesn't have that effect on me," I add.

"That's fine," she says, "as long as you don't scoff at other people's fascination with numbers. Math is just as important as English. Numbers, like language, provide one with a way to arrange the world's chaos. They are two kinds of truths, and science and history and art and psychology are other truths. The world is chaos, Alex. Your job in life is to figure out how to make some sense of the chaos. Me, I do it through words. Maybe that's why I won this award. Maybe that's what my professors were trying to tell me."

Pause. The lights are buzzing over our heads. She says, "I hate fluorescent lights, don't you?" As if she knows that I have given these lights some thought, as if we are on the same page.

"Oh, yeah." I nod. "They're so . . . they're so . . ."

"Heartless." She finishes my sentence for me.

Same word, same page, same feeling, same everything. Haley and me, me and Haley.

Fifth- and Sixth-Form Parents' Weekend

Letter in the mailbox from Dad. He writes me every week. I'm a less regular correspondent, though I do make the obligatory call every couple of days, a two-minute conversation just so he can hear my voice. Dad will not be coming this weekend. I've known this for a long time, and it's fine. Except for this semester, I see him regularly because he lives close by. But he has to make a living to support me, and in his field, making a living means taking a sabbatical when it's offered so that you have time to write a book and be published and bring honor and glory to the university where you teach. That is why my dad isn't coming.

I don't know about my mom. I talked to her the day after the accident, but I haven't heard from her since. I hope she doesn't come. She is very beautiful but strange. Before she married my dad, she lived in London and went on some dates with Mick Jagger, a fact I let slip during my first month at Birch because I knew it would buy me clout. If she comes to Parents' Weekend, she will wear something crazy, like a dashiki or red high-heeled shoes. She will be labeled by my friends as a Fum (boarding-school speak for "f^ckable mom").

No letter in the mailbox from Thomas's parents, of course, because they will have just gotten mine.

On Parents' Weekend, a fountain will be unveiled in the center of the quad. It will be dedicated to the memory of Thomas Broughton, class of 1984, given by the parents of the class of 1984. Is this some kind of symbol or cautionary reminder? Did anyone think this through? A fountain???!!! I bet you money that Thomas wants nothing to do with water, not to mention with the class of 1984.

New and Improved Homework (the Rough Draft)

Ginger Rogers

He was such a bad monkey that I had to stuff him into my suitcase and take him to the train station and leave him there for some other little girl to find. He had only been with me for two days, and already, he needed a reform school or a new family with much wider boundaries.

At the yard sale, he had looked so festive with his red mouth and red ball on top of his cap. A little cherry of a ball. His mouth did not open, and he had big ears, which made him the perfect companion for me because I am such a talker. But my mother did not know when she bought him for a quarter that he talked, too. He talked to me in his dreams.

Sometimes I was a part of his dream. Sometimes, in the dream, he was big and I was small. Sometimes he carried me by his right hand, swinging me down the sidewalks of Dreamland. He never dropped me, but once, he threw me up into a tree, where I had to hang by my toes for seven hours, which was much worse than being dropped. Once, he made a boat for me out of sticks and leaves and pushed me over a waterfall. I survived, but barely.

I could hear the monkey knocking against the suitcase. He was tap dancing. He thought he was a fabulous tap dancer, but I had news for him: he was no Fred Astaire. "Stop being so bad!" I yelled through the keyhole.

"I'll stop being bad when you give me a name," he yelled back.

"Don't you sass me, Bad Monkey," I said.

"I am magic," he whispered. "Don't you get it? If you name me, all your troubles will be over. Please give me a name, and don't leave me here in this dirty train station all alone."

So I sat down on a bench and unlocked the suitcase. "Fred," I said, pulling him to me and hugging him tight. "You are such a Fred."

The Artist vs. the Barbarian

When Miss Dovecott reads my charmingly quirky, symbolic-sounding but utterly pointless story, maybe she will fall in love with me all over again. And maybe she will forgive me for all that I am about to do, for all I have already done. Who ain't a slave? Tell me that.

I thought I would sail about a little and see the watery part of the world.

SATURDAY, OCTOBER 21, 12:35 P.M.

Running, Yesterday

It is the time of day when the sun turns treetops into keepers of light. After redoing my homework and leaving it on Miss Dovecott's desk, I run through that light, up one side of the hill and down the other, imagining possibilities. . . . Miss Dovecott is only five years older than I am, and in five years, when I'm out of college and the age difference won't matter, we can fall in love properly and go to restaurants and drink wine and whisper into each other's eyes and get married and live in an apartment with fresh flowers on every table and bookshelf, flowers that I select myself and bring home from the corner market.

The wildflowers that grow on the banks of the French Broad River have all gone under the earth. Like Thomas. It is a Friday with no rain. The sun leaves nothing of itself on the water; cold air raises goose bumps on my legs. Birds skim

93

across the path, leaves murmur beneath my shoes, sounds that become one with the river.

I stand on a bank far away from the headwaters, far away from the rock. The water is gray but inviting because it is moving, going somewhere. I step down into it, and it covers my shoes and socks. Cold, cold. I take another step, then another. I am up to my knees in water. I test myself to see how far I can go: top of my shorts, my balls start shriveling; up to my belly button; my gray shirt sucks up the gray water, turning my shirt darker. I make it up to my neck, and then it's too much. I flounder back up the bank, where I fold into myself to stay warm, rocking back and forth to the pulse of the river until my heartbeat falls in unison with it.

"Oh, Alex, it's you," a voice says, and I jump.

When I turn my head around, Miss Dovecott steps toward me, her eyes flickering with curiosity. She must wonder what I am doing here when most guys are having dinner with their parents.

"You're all wet," she says.

"Yes, ma'am."

"Why would you want to go swimming on a day like today?"

"Uh . . ." I don't have an answer.

"You're cold."

"I just finished running."

"You should dry off."

I take off my shirt.

"You're shaking," she says. When she pulls her sweatshirt over her head, I see her nipples poking through her bra and into her shirt. "Here. You need this more than I do."

"No, I don't."

"Yes, you do. I'm fine. I have on a turtleneck."

"I don't need your sweatshirt, Miss Dovecott."

"Alex, the tips of your fingers are blue."

I lift my hands to look at them. She holds the sweatshirt out to me, and I take it, putting my arms through the sleeves, then pulling it over my head in one quick motion. On Miss Dovecott the sweatshirt is miniskirt length, but it fits me.

"I'm on my way back up to campus," she says. "Want to join me?"

I nod and follow.

"I heard the cross-country team won the other day," she says. "And a personal best for you. Congratulations."

(I didn't have time to write about it here in this book.)

"Thanks." I smile, curious. "Who told you?"

"Mr. Wellfleet. He was proud."

"Yeah, he was jumping around all over the place. You'd have thought we'd won the Olympics or something."

Because the path is narrow, I let her walk in front. To talk face to face is impossible, and sending small talk into the back of her head feels pointless. I try not to stare at her bottom in case she suddenly turns around.

I suppress the urge to grab her by the waist and instead tap her on the shoulder. "I know a shortcut," I say, stepping in front of her, wondering if she might be studying the muscles in my calves or the mud spattered on the back of them. As we angle away from the rush of the river, I pick up the pace. When the path disappears, I lead her over cushions of leaves, weaving in and out of trees. We are almost running, but she has no trouble keeping up, and I don't slow down until I reach the sycamore with the low, oblong knothole. "The coolest tree on campus," I say. I press my hand on the trunk next to the hole. "Once I found a bird's nest here."

I do not say that when I went running for help on the day Thomas died, I stopped here on the way up the hill to the infirmary, out of my mind with panic, and sobbed for at least two minutes.

A single bird whisks by over our heads, and we look up. The light is gone from the treetops, leaving only feathers of cloud in the sky. I take the opportunity to earn a few brownie points. "I've been meaning to ask if you could recommend a book for me to read. Anything you think I might like that isn't too 'Englishy.' You know what I mean. I like English. It's my favorite class. It really is; I'm not just saying that."

She smiles. "Well, have you read *Crime and Punishment*?"

"I've seen it on my dad's bookshelf at home." I pause. "But to be honest, it looks kind of long, and I don't have a lot of extra reading time." I do not tell her that I'm in the process of slogging through *Moby-Dick* because at the rate I'm going, I may not make it all the way. "Can you think of something a little shorter?"

"Why don't you try *In Our Time,* by Hemingway? It's a collection of stories about a young man named Nick Adams, a soldier in World War I. I'm sure the library has a copy. If not, you're welcome to borrow mine."

By now we have reached the top of the hill, where below us the school buildings cast their long shadows. A game of touch football has started in the quad, but it is too far away for me to make out the players. I feel empty, a whole Friday night without study hall stretching before me, and I almost ask Miss Dovecott if she wants to drive into town for dinner. I consider offering an observation about dark closing in on us, but that sounds stupid, too. I am almost expecting her to say something about Thomas, to pounce and try to draw the truth out of me, like a mouth on a rattlesnake bite, but she doesn't. What she says is "I'm taking you to the infirmary."

For a split second, I think she means her apartment, but then I realize she is worried that I might have hypothermia. When I check in with Nurse Patty, I am still wearing Miss Dovecott's sweatshirt.

Ice Cream

In the waiting room with its clanking radiator, Nurse Patty gives me some towels and checks my temperature. Normal. She makes me drink tea from a china cup with pink roses on it, then sends me back to my dorm to shower in time for dinner. I stuff the damp sweatshirt under my bed for the time being, throw on khakis and a collared shirt, and run to the dining hall for make-'em-yourself sundaes, cold comfort for the parentless. I eat three of them, and they actually do make me feel better for a little while. I sit at the corner table usually occupied by faculty, where the tall windows come together, and I look through my own reflection out into the night, where things I know nothing about are happening. Afterward, in the darkness of my room, I lie on my bed naked with the sweatshirt in my arms, aching all over.

Old Man

The next morning (this morning) at the library, I find *In Our Time,* right where it should be, and I sit in my carrel for forty-five minutes, reading. I have a Latin quiz first period (yes, they still make us go to Saturday class even on Parents' Weekend) that I should be studying for, but I'm not interested in Latin right now. I am Nick Adams, the soldier who has to keep his mind shut down in order to get through a day.

By the time the bell rings, the scent of the book has worked its way into the creases of my palms. It is a nice smell, really, a grandfather's-closet smell, and I am smiling as I walk to the circulation desk even though I am about to fail a quiz. I pull the card out of the back of the Hemingway book and sign my name. That's when I see another name. Thomas Broughton checked out this book in March of 1956. Quick as a wink, I erase my name from the card, but the eraser smudges rather than clears, and I can still see my handwriting. I reach across the circulation desk to grab a black felt-tip pen, and I color in the whole block so that no trace of my name remains. I return the book to the shelf where it belongs and check out *The Old Man and the Sea* instead.

SUNDAY, OCTOBER 22, 9:15 A.M.

Saturday Night at Boarding School on Parents' Weekend

You don't have a lot of options. You don't want to be the only guy on dorm other than the shy Korean kid whose family lives halfway around the world. You don't want to feel sorry for yourself as you sit and watch girl shows like *The Love Boat* and *Fantasy Island*. You think you might sail about a little and see the watery part of the world; you think you might sign up for the mixer designed to keep the under-formers occupied and the upper-form losers like you and the Korean kid from killing yourselves. Sure enough, the evening doesn't seem nearly as bleak when you see who the chaperone is. You tuck a paperback into your jacket pocket just in case you and she want to get literary.

The Mixer

I am one in a trail of boys streaming from the Birch School bus across the well-lit courtyard of St. Brigid, a girls' school seventy miles away. At the table inside the heavy glass doors of the gym, two smiling middle-aged women wearing earplugs hand out name tags and markers. There are rules here (there are rules everywhere we ever go on a bus): no kissing on the dance floor, for example, and no one leaves the gym until eleven o'clock, when it's time to get back on the bus. Only three hours to get down to the business of mixers, which is to get at least to second base, but I'm not in the mood. I find a corner with some light and remove Hemingway from the pocket of my sports coat. I scan the room for Miss Dovecott. She is standing with the other chaperones, some of them male—there are two other boys' schools here—so I look around for anyone I know. Too dark. I decide to make a circle around the hardwood floor so maybe Miss Dovecott will take note of my swinging-single self.

In the middle of a crowd of dancers, a couple is kissing, seeing how long they can get away with it. The loud music precludes any sort of talking I might want to do with a St. Brigid girl, the well-groomed Ivory-soap type. When I bend down for a sip at the water fountain, someone taps me on the shoulder. It's one of the Ivory girls, a small, gawky one. A couple of her friends are pointing at me and shaking their hips in time to the song, "Get Down Tonight," by KC & the Sunshine Band. "Would you like to dance?" she squeaks.

As horny as I am, I draw the line at girls who look twelve, have braces, and sound like Minnie Mouse. I tell Minnie I'm not feeling well. She nods. As I hurry away in the opposite direction, I slip, my ankle twisting in the penny loafers I am not used to, and even though the music is loud, I hear the girls' mocking laughter, amplified for my benefit to show that they have gotten over being rejected by Goofy. I climb into a dark row of bleachers and watch Minnie and friends disappear into the crowd in the middle of the dance floor, where boys and girls become indistinguishable, faces bobbing up and down like part of a giant machine. I am playing it cool, but I sure as hell don't feel it.

In a way, it isn't that cool to go to mixers because it means you don't have a girlfriend back home. It is fine if you're a new boy, but after that, not nearly as cool, although you redeem yourself ever so slightly if you hook up with a fox or if your girlfriend attends the boarding school and you hang out with her all night in the bushes. Joe Bonnin has a younger sister at St. Brigid, and I wonder if I should go look for her. But what do I do if I find her? She's not that foxy. I check my watch—8:36—and scan the room. When I see who is coming my way, I pull out *The Old Man and the Sea*, book in one hand, sore ankle in the other. I am massaging it absentmindedly when Miss Dovecott sits down.

"Too much dancing already?" she says.

I laugh and tell her I tripped.

"Do you think you sprained it?"

"No, no," I say, "it's not that bad. Just twisted it. I'm kind of clumsy."

She is smiling at me. "Have you started *In Our Time* yet?"

I lift up my paperback. "I couldn't find it in the library, so I tried this one."

"You can borrow my copy, then."

"That would be great," I say, and she smiles. "Hey, why aren't you dancing?"

"That's really not my job here tonight, is it?"

"I don't know. Aren't chaperones allowed a little fun every now and then?"

"To tell you the truth, I'm not a very good dancer."

"Join the club."

"What club is that?"

I pause, then shrug. "I don't know, whatever you call the People Who Can't Dance Club."

"I think we can come up with a better name than that."

"Okay. You go first."

Miss Dovecott laughs. "You're the creative one around here."

"But you're smarter than I am. You went to Princeton." And my mind flashes to her sweatshirt tucked away in my room. "By the way, thank you for lending me your sweatshirt. I'll return it to you after I wash it."

"That'll be fine," she says.

And then, I go for it. "I liked wearing it," I say.

She looks down at her feet and changes the subject. "Well, back to chaperoning."

"Is it as boring as it looks?"

"Never boring," she says. "Too many people to watch and talk to. Just a few minutes ago, the chaperone from St. Mark's was telling me about a suicide at their school your freshman year."

"Yeah, we had an assembly about it."

"This teacher's theory is that the boy took all those pills because he was struggling with his sexuality." She pauses. "He might have been gay."

"Huh," I say, "they didn't tell us that part. But you know how it is at boarding schools."

"No, I didn't go to one. How is it?"

"Rumor Central."

"Well, any closed community is that way."

"Was it like that at Princeton?"

"Are you trying to change the subject?"

"What subject?"

"You know, Alex, I have a theory."

"Shoot."

"My theory is that you boys plaster your walls with pin-ups because you feel the need to present yourselves as heterosexual."

"Go on."

"And, statistically, there has to be a small percentage of gay students at Birch."

"Look, Miss Dovecott. Here's the thing. If you go to a boys' boarding school, people who don't know the culture think you're either gay or a troublemaker. I get tired of explaining that I don't go to a military academy and that I'm not being punished for anything. Like this mother at the pool where I worked last summer, when she found out I went to Birch, she said, 'Well, you don't seem like a bad kid.'"

"I know you're not a bad kid."

"But maybe I am. Maybe I ought to be at a military academy."

"Why do you say that, Alex?"

"Because. Because I think I might feel better if somebody kicked my ass."

"You feel guilty about Thomas," she says.

"You're damn right I do," I say, and I sling *The Old Man and the Sea* to the darkest corner of the bleachers. "But I don't want to talk about it, not with you, not with anybody."

"I think I know why."

I look at her sideways.

"Because the whole story hasn't come to light yet."

I am about to shit my pants, but I hear Glenn's voice calming me down. Cool it, Stromm, cool it. "I'm not sure I follow you," I say.

"I think we should wait and talk about this at school with Mr. Parkes, don't you?" Miss Dovecott rises, looking in the direction of where I threw the book. "Before you get back on the bus," she says, "make sure you pick up after yourself."

Green Fields

My freshman year, the only thing I ever did at the river was wade into it and fish. The fact that it could be used for jumping into, for drinking alongside of, did not occur to me. Vodka? I barely knew it existed; my dad drank beer, and not even very much of it. I knew Michelangelo and Andy Warhol existed, Monet and Manet, and I was tested on the difference between them, but if you had asked me the difference between Jack Daniel's and Jim Beam, I would have said one played baseball and the other basketball.

Glenn and I were paired together about a month into school by our art appreciation teacher to do a presentation on Jan Vermeer (an artist we should appreciate). I owe my friendship with Glenn to Vermeer because it was after that that Glenn took me in. He thought I was smarter than anyone else in the class. He couldn't believe the stuff I noticed in the paintings, like how Vermeer painted a story behind the scene by inserting a single suggestion of movement in the stillness. I actually appreciated Vermeer, but I was not a fan of Monet or the impressionists—all that haze and suggestion. Glenn agreed wholeheartedly. He invited me swimming one night when there was Open Swim at the indoor pool, and we played water tag and Marco Polo with some other guys, and we all took turns doing silly jumps and dives off the board. Glenn was nicer back then, when he wasn't suspicious of everybody and everything.

At the time, I didn't know about all the bad things that water could hide. I considered water as something that made me feel otherworldly, like a dolphin or a sea turtle on a very long journey. Back when I had never even heard of this school, it was easy to pretend that the deep end of the public swimming pool was the Pacific Ocean.

The old man and the sea. The boy and the river. I can pretend all I want, but the fact is, I will never finish this book.

There now is your insular city of the Manhattoes.

Who the hell are the Manhattoes, *Her*-man? Did you make them up? Are they a tribe of crazies who live on some island? I live on an island. Hell, I *am* an island. I am a rock.

But a rock does feel pain. And an island cries often in the privacy of his own room. I am a big fan of Simon and Garfunkel, thanks to my dad; I grew up listening to their melancholy strains. Today's pop music doesn't interest me. Foreigner? REO Speedwagon? Give me a break.

Campus at one a.m. when almost no one is here is just plain weird. As the bus rolls up the drive, the cluster of stone buildings looks like the set of a horror movie—a sequel to *The Shining,* which is a damn scary movie. There now is your Insular City of Man. Mist shrouds the grass. The lamps along the sidewalk look disembodied from their posts, fuzzy balls of light, just enough to see by.

In my room, the books I left stacked on my desk have

105

something to say, but they aren't talking. The photograph of me and my dad with our arms roped over one another's shoulders was taken a lifetime ago. There is a fly at the window beating its brains against the glass. Poems buzz behind my worn-out eyes, but I don't want to think about poems anymore, I don't want to think about what my English teacher might have seen us doing at the river. I want to sleep with Haley's sweatshirt. I want to sleep with Haley. I put on Simon and Garfunkel's *Greatest Hits* album, and like a bridge over troubled water, I lay me down and picture the way I would touch her waist, trace the curve of her shoulders, put my mouth on her lips, her neck, her breasts, and, gently, within the sounds of silence, push inside her.

Faraway Betty

After his parents drop him back on campus late this morning, Glenn knocks on my door. I am at my desk, struggling with trigonometric equations.

"We were looking for you," he says. "My mom and dad wanted to say hey."

"I must have been in the library," I say.

"I saw Miss Dovecott just now," he tells me.

"Well, whoop-dee-friggin'-doo. I just saw Mr. Parkes." I stopped by his apartment because I was afraid if I didn't, Miss Dovecott would arrange a meeting for the three of us to talk about the day at the river. As they say, the best defense is a good offense: I told my advisor that I'd been feeling guilty but that I was working it out for myself on paper, which was helping a lot, and I needed time before I talked about it with anyone other than Reverend Black, but I did want to talk about it with Mr. Parkes eventually, and I would let him know when I was ready.

"Yeah, so your girlfriend was in her classroom. I hope you don't mind; I just stopped in to say hello."

"Glenn," I say, "what did you do?"

"Nothing, I swear. I just popped in to ask how she was doing. You know, up close, she's not all that good-looking. She's a Faraway Betty."

"Whatever you say."

"And she smells like mothballs."

"It's probably her sweater."

"Have you ever noticed," says Glenn, "how she dresses like a college student trying to pass herself off as a teacher?"

"Nope." But I had noticed that her outfits were slightly out of whack—a button-down shirt and wrinkled khakis with a silk scarf or a string of pearls.

"I bet she's a lesbian," Glenn says.

"Get over yourself."

"She dresses like a man. Most lesbos do."

"Yeah, like you know a lot of lesbians."

"I do, as a matter of fact. My mom's best friend is a lesbian."

"Maybe your mom's a lesbian, too."

"In your dreams."

"Everson," I say, "I can honestly say that I have never, ever dreamed about your mother." She has bouffant hair and wears lots of gold jewelry.

"Well, I can't say the same about yours. She's a Fum." (See? I told you.)

"Get out."

"I never finished telling you what happened that night when I went for help on the Roethke poem."

"So tell me."

"She put her hand on my knee. When we were sitting there. She reached over and put her creepy lesbo hand on my knee."

"You are such a liar."

"I reported her," Glenn said.

"What?"

"To Dean Mansfield."

I am standing now. "Oh, my God. What were you thinking?"

"At least one of us is thinking."

"He's going to know you're lying, and then we are screwed. He's not going to take your word over a teacher's."

"Wanna bet?"

"I am out, Glenn. Seriously, leave me out of this."

"Have you done the English homework for tomorrow?" I haven't. "She's smoking us out, Stromm. Miss Dovecott knows. You'll see what I mean. The poem for Monday isn't even in our book. Stevie Smith is British, not American. And a chick—probably a lesbo, with a name like Stevie. Which obviously Miss D failed to mention."

"How do you know that?"

"I looked it up," Glenn says. "In the *Dictionary of Literary Biography*. This is an American literature class, remember? Why would she have us read an English poem?"

"How should I know?"

"You're the Poet Boy."

"Leave, please."

"Just wait. You'll see what I mean."

I don't tell Glenn what Miss Dovecott said to me at the mixer—I never even tell him I went to the mixer in the first place—and I don't read the poem on the handout until just now. "Not Waving but Drowning," it's called, about a man who drowns, but his friends think he's waving. I try to hold my pen straight as I answer the questions asked of me. I try not to read the poem too many times because if I do, it will worm its sneaky way into my heart.

MONDAY, OCTOBER 23, 7:45 P.M.

English Homework

Miss Dovecott is standing at her classroom door this morning as we file in from assembly. I swear to God she is watching my hands, staring at them like they are foreign things not attached to my arms. I steady my page of notebook paper for her to take and do not look her in the eye.

We expect her to go over the Stevie Smith poem, but instead she hands out a copy of a poem that a friend of hers from college wrote called "Superman Laments His X-Ray Vision." It makes me laugh out loud; Superman walks around the city wishing he couldn't see through ladies' bras and underwear. And it makes me sad, too, when Superman starts wishing that he didn't have the ability to see inside people's souls because there is too much in need of saving there, and one person, even a superhero, can't possibly do all that.

I think it's cool that a college student wrote it, and I think it's even cooler that Miss Dovecott shows it to us. She compares it to Holden Caulfield's realization in *The Catcher in the Rye,* and at that point, I tune out and focus on undressing Miss Dovecott with my X-ray vision.

Green Fields

I fondled a girl's breasts once. Her nipples were tiny, but her tits were huge. They took up the whole top half of her, and I swear she would have let me have the bottom half, too, if my dad and her parents (also university professors) hadn't been on the other side of the sliding glass doors. We sat on the side of her swimming pool with our shorts on, our backs to the house, our feet in the water. She told me my tanned legs were sexy. It was summer, and the girl, a year older, was home from boarding school—Foxcroft. She was wearing a sweatshirt that did not reveal, until she removed it, how stacked she was. I almost couldn't breathe. She laid the sweatshirt across my crotch and slid a hand underneath it. She put her other hand across my mouth when I moaned and came in my shorts. Before we went inside for dessert, I spilled a Coke down my front on purpose to cover up what else was there, and the whole rest of the night I worried that I'd gotten some of it on her sweatshirt.

The Sweatshirt

I have been hiding it in the bottom drawer of Clay's empty dresser because it feels like I have stolen it. Something in me doesn't want to give it back. It could be a simple process, really—just put it on her desk when no one is looking. I saw her wear the sweatshirt once when she was on her way down to the soccer field. She worked out with the team every now and then. She never knew I was watching her, but the whole time, she was constantly—or is it continually? I've never gotten those two adverbs straight—adjusting her shorts, rolling them up at the waist, then rolling them back down again, trying to decide, I guess, if she was showing too much leg or not. She opted for more leg than less, and why shouldn't she? But most of her clothes, like her sweatshirt, are baggy.

After class today, I take a long whiff of the gray cotton fabric just as Glenn bursts into the room. "Stromm, what are you doing?"

I shrug and hold it up for him to see.

"'Princeton,'" he reads. "I didn't know you got in early."

"Ha, ha." And I tell him some of the story of how I got the sweatshirt.

"Why didn't you tell me you had it?" Glenn asks, as calm as ever. "We can use it against her."

"I was going to wrap it up and give it to you for Christmas."

"F^ck you."

"You wish," I say.

"What's that supposed to mean?"

"Nothing."

"You know what, Stromm? I don't trust you."

"I don't trust me, either," I say. "I don't like what we're doing to Miss Dovecott. I don't like The Plan." I pause. "Did she really put her hand on your knee?"

"Yep," Glenn says.

"But she didn't mean anything by it."

"I think she did."

"You think she's a lesbian. Why would a lesbian put her hand on your knee? She was being motherly."

"She was coming on to me, just like she's come on to you." He pauses. "Are you jealous? You look green."

"Of course I'm not jealous," I say. But I am.

"We've got to keep her off balance," Glenn says. "I'm doing my part. I unsettle her, and you get close. So get close."

"How much closer do you expect me to get?"

"Alex," Glenn says. "Come on. Now I've got to go to practice, and so do you. And do something about these walls. This room is depressing as hell."

Is hell depressing? I doubt it, I bet it shoots you full of speed, I bet you are forever up and running for your life, which is to say your death. Before I leave for practice, I stuff the sweatshirt into the bottom of my laundry bag. If Glenn comes back to steal it, he might think to look there, but at least he'll have to comb through plenty of dirty underwear and socks to get to it.

It is a damp, drizzly November in my soul.

/

WEDNESDAY, OCTOBER 25, 9:20 P.M.

Boarding-school calendar: September, low because summer's over; October, higher because the sky is so clear and blue. November, low; December, high because we're away from school for half of it. January, lower than September and November combined; February, lower still. March, high because of spring break; April, higher—the end is in sight; May, even higher. June, the highest, high as a kite.

We never do go over the Stevie Smith poem, but the story about the monkey is returned to me with the words "See me" written across the top. See me. *Miss Dovecott, I see you all the time, in my mind, in the clouds, in the trees, in my dreams. I am always seeing you.*

Seeing Her

When I walk into her classroom after school today, she smiles. She hands me a sheet of paper announcing a nationwide literary essay contest for high-school juniors and seniors; she wants me to submit something. I say sure, why not, and she smiles even wider. Then, THEN, she asks me to tell her a little more about myself, stuff she may not know, so that she can write the recommendation that goes with the essay.

So I tell her a little about my dad and his European background.

"I've been to Europe," Miss Dovecott says. "Two summers ago. My mom and I went. We did the whole 'art in Europe' tour. In Florence, we stayed in a very old convent smack in the middle of everything. You should go someday."

With you, I am thinking. Let me go there with you. Instead I ask, "So, what was the convent like?"

Sitting at her desk, she leans forward on her elbows. "It was the most perfect place. We had a window that reached from the floor to the ceiling. I think I could have stood at that window for the rest of my life."

"I like windows, too." God, I sound stupid.

"Have you traveled abroad, Alex?"

"No, ma'am."

"Maybe you should think about going on one of the summer programs with Birch to Spain or France."

"I take Latin. There's no place to go for that."

"There's the art trip to Italy over spring break. They used to speak Latin there." She smiles. "And you would get to see Florence."

"I'm not sure my dad can afford it," I say.

"I wish I could take you," she says.

My eyes open wide. "You do?"

"Sure. I was a scholarship student at Princeton, so I understand where you're coming from."

"I wish you could take me, too."

"Well, maybe someday." She smiles an enigmatic Emily Dickinson smile. Is she flirting with me? I think she is flirting with me. I don't know what to say next, so I ramble.

"My dad will be happy that you are having me enter this contest. What should I write about?" I look down at the flyer she has handed me and read from it. " 'Literary essay.' Like the ones we write in class?"

"Not exactly. More like an artful narrative. A more polished version of your 'What I Carry' essay, for example. You could even use that one."

"I don't want to use that one," I say. "Give me another idea."

She plays with her watch, and then I see her see something in her head that will make sense to me.

"In Florence, one morning after breakfast—we had breakfast on the balcony, strong Italian coffee and hard rolls and butter, very simple, everything was so simple there—anyway, one morning after breakfast, I was standing at the window looking down at the street, and I saw a girl—a young woman—who looked just like me. She walked like me; her hair was the same color, the same length. And she was looking up just as I was looking down. We both froze."

I am right there with her, face to the glass. "Then what?"

"Well, I put my palm up to the window. I remember thinking that it was like that moment in *Romeo and Juliet* when they first talk to each other, palm to palm, the holy palmers' kiss. 'If I profane with my unworthiest hand/This holy shrine.' Do you know that part?" I don't, but I nod anyway. "Then the girl on the street did the same thing, put her palm up. All of a sudden, the sun, which had been behind a cloud, washed over her face, blanking it out like a canvas. All I could see was her palm. It felt as if she were blessing me."

"Weird," I say, still nodding.

"It *was* weird," she says. "I'd never felt this before, and this will sound crazy to you because it is—crazy—but I thought this girl, this woman, might have been God. I ran out of my room, down the stairs, but when I got to the street, I couldn't find her. I stood there in her spot for a few minutes, hoping she might come back. She didn't." Miss Dovecott stares at me like I have some kind of psychic insight. I don't.

"That's too bad," I say.

She leans toward me across the plane of birch or whatever wood her desk is made of. "But here's the really freaky part. As I was standing there on the street, I looked up at the window, *my* window, and I realized she hadn't been able to see me at all. There was a glare. She hadn't been able to see anything. I had washed my nightgown out in the sink and had hung it right next to the window to dry, and I couldn't even see that."

She goes on about something else, but I am stuck on the wet nightgown. I can see her in it, standing on a balcony in the Italian sunshine, damp with desire.

THURSDAY, OCTOBER 26, 7:15 A.M.

Seeing Glenn

I knock on his door, the door that used to be Thomas's door, too, Wednesday night. He isn't there. I am ready to tell him that I want out. But it is too late to get out. I know it, and

Glenn knows it. I hate myself for agreeing to The Plan. I hate myself for reeling Miss Dovecott into my heart even though I want her there, and I hate her for allowing it. I hate myself for what I will tell Glenn when I see him. I hate myself for all that I know.

Rock, Paper, Scissors

Thomas does hit his head on a rock when he dives into the river. He does lose consciousness, he does sink, and Glenn and I do pull him to shore. When I try to do CPR one last time, Glenn pushes me off Thomas and pulls me up so he can look at me straight on. "He's dead, Alex." I kneel back down and grab Thomas's wrist, searching for a pulse. I feel nothing, and I take Thomas's hand in mine and hold it there.

But still, I'm not so sure he's dead. I mean, I think he is. I'm 99 percent sure. Maybe it's wishful thinking, or a flash of last sun through the treetops, or Glenn's shadow standing over us, maybe it's even magic, but I think I see Thomas's eyelid flutter.

Glenn says he doesn't see it. He says what I see is due to panic and a million other emotions flashing through my heart at a hundred miles per hour. He says that we have done all we can do, that he'll run up to the infirmary while I wait with the body. "I'll be back," he says, and then he grabs my shoulder. "Wait. No, you go; you're faster. I'll stay here." What he does see is me take off running, full of breath, seconds before, from the other direction, Miss Dovecott comes upon the scene, breathless.

117

More Running

There is a lot to be said for running. It is an in-between place. It's not like you're touching the sky, but sometimes, if you are in the zone, you feel like you could. And when you are finished running, there is a wide, clean column of air all the way through the inside of your body.

Like at today's meet in Asheville, I come in second. It feels like hope to mount the hill on wings of eagles, as Mr. Wellfleet puts it, to run and run and not be weary. The course at St. John's School concludes at the top of a hill, which is different from most courses, and winds its way there between cow pastures. The cows run, too, when they see me coming, and it makes me laugh, how the calves buck along behind their mothers, though it seems to me that they would rather linger by the fence and blink their eyes in the breeze as I sweep by. At some point, I decide I will pass all the runners ahead of me, I will overtake them one by one, and as we head up the hill to the finish, there is only one guy I don't catch, but if the course had been a bus length longer, I would have.

It is another personal best for me, and to celebrate, Mr. Wellfleet takes the whole team to dinner at the mall on the way back to school, where we gather at the center of the food court and talk our coach into giving us fifteen minutes of shopping. Most of us go into Spencer's Gifts, the shop with the erection pills and other jokes for men turning fifty, and the black lights and the posters. When we see the one of Cheryl Tiegs in her see-through swimsuit, two of the guys on the team tell me they never cared much for Clay, and I tell them I didn't care much for him, either. They are all talking to me like I'm normal again, but maybe that's because I'm smiling, really smiling, for the first time in nearly a month. With allowance money from my dad, I buy a poster of Albert Einstein with his hair gone wild, and I rush out to the bus, high on the day's victories.

I am feeling good until I set foot on campus again, and the gray haze descends. Glenn is walking to the gym when I get off the bus. We wave to each other across the dark. On my way back to dorm, I stop by the library for a visit with *Moby-Dick*. All of these words keeping me afloat.

SATURDAY, OCTOBER 28, 8:05 P.M.

The Archives Room

Down, down, down. This is where we go this morning for English class, into the basement of the main building, to the school archives. Air-raid drills, gas rations, and no away games, a historic touchdown pass late in the fourth quarter by a guy who went off to fight with his older brother and never came home. A beloved teacher who once organized all his history students to write weekly letters to Birch alums in uniform overseas. The Birch School archives are about war.

Miss Dovecott asks us to poke around, to find one point of reflection and write a poem that illustrates that journey of reflection. I am still half-asleep. I look at Glenn, who has taken a yearbook from the shelf and is curled into one of the reading chairs. He looks peaceful.

I pick up an old school newspaper from April of 1956. My stomach drops to the floor when I see the lead article about a drowning at the river. A boy went swimming

119

alone, a sad-looking boy named Clark Keever. Surely Thomas Broughton, Senior, reader of Hemingway, knew him, at least passed by him on the brick sidewalks. Did he think of Clark Keever this past month, remembering? I close the newspaper with its distant smell and put it back on the shelf where it belongs.

I study Miss Dovecott, who is helping Joe Bonnin. In one corner of the Archives Room is a tribute to all of the Birch boys who fought for their country. This one guy in the class of '39 who died at Guadalcanal, during his short life, discovered a species of butterfly that now bears his name. That is what I choose to reflect on, not the drowned boy. The title of my reflection is not very original—"Butterfly"—but maybe there's something to the poem.

Death hung your photograph on the wall
as smooth and taut as the sheet laid across your body,
November 1942. Forty years later I study your face,
dig up scrapbooks, newspapers, to find your life.
You were senior prefect, yearbook editor;
you set off for Princeton as a prince.
When did you have time to discover anything?

You must have waded some black primeval swamp,
you, who led your high school classmates,
broke Ivy League records in scholarship and sport,
you, who enlisted April of your junior year.
So when did you spot this winged
Appias drusilla boydi that, before you,
lived unnoticed and unnamed?
When did you have time

120

to track a bright, uncocooned thing
in the damp and darkening air?

Before dinner, I knock on Glenn's door. For the first time, we talk about something other than Thomas, other than Miss Dovecott. We talk about the Archives Room. He has chosen to write about his father, a graduate of the class of 1950. The yearbook was dedicated to him, Glenn Albright Everson II. He saved the life of a faculty child who had fallen on a nest of yellow jackets and would have surely died, given the number of stings. When Glenn is telling me that his father never told him this, I hear tears in his voice. It is a damp and drizzly November in my soul, and I want to cry, too, for this man who built a fire in the fireplace for a boy one Thanksgiving, for this man who is more golden than his son, but there isn't time to cry. The six o'clock bell is ringing.

SUNDAY, OCTOBER 29, 9:02 A.M.

Insomnia on the High Seas

Maybe Is Male was born too late. Like Glenn's sister said, he is an old soul. He could have been friends with Glenn's father rather than with Glenn. For the first time in his life, Is Male prays. He is so tired of not sleeping. His bunk mate, who was thrown overboard by the captain, left his Bible behind. Is Male picks it up, turns to the index, reads all the verses pertaining to guilt. This is how he finds Psalm 32, the dyslexic's Psalm 23. In Is Male's heathen opinion, Psalm 32 blows Psalm 23 out of the water, especially verse 3: "When I kept silence, my bones waxed old through my roaring all the day long." That's it, Is Male says out loud to no one. Then,

121

verse 4—"For day and night thy hand was heavy upon me: my moisture is turned into the drought of summer." It is true, Is Male thinks: the weight of his deed has shriveled up every good thing. "Compass me about with songs of deliverance," says the permanent ink of Psalm 32. It is a big job, Is Male tells God; if You exist, I hope You're up to the task.

Posted like silent sentinels all around the town, stand thousands upon thousands of mortal men fixed in ocean reveries.

SUNDAY, OCTOBER 29, 8:36 P.M.

The Day Before Thomas Died

It was a Friday, exactly one month ago. I had a huge history test on colonial America first thing that morning, and I studied for it right through breakfast.

Clay didn't make his bed or empty his trash, so his name got posted on the demerit sheet.

I ate lunch with a table full of guys.

It had rained Thursday night, and the cross-country team had to run through mud.

The dining hall served fried flounder for dinner.

I studied for a Latin quiz and wrote up my chemistry lab report. I'm sure I did my English homework, too.

Glenn and Thomas came to our room after the Lights-Out bell (which is allowed on the weekends, visiting until midnight). We set the time for the next day, and where we would meet. Thomas told a stupid (but funny) joke about a mouse f^cking a giraffe. We laughed about what had happened the night before, when Andy had dared Joe to try the new hot sauce in the dining hall, and Joe did, putting a drop on his index finger, licking it, and then forgetting to wash his hands. When he went to relieve himself during study hall that night, he rushed out of the dorm bathroom screaming that his penis was on fire. It was hilarious, and even now, it makes me smile.

That night before I fell asleep, I remember thinking how the outside world was so far away. Only the teachers kept up with the news; if they were to ask me, for example, what was happening in the Soviet Union, I wouldn't have been able to answer. Sad to say, but true: most of us only care about ourselves, as you can tell by the self-absorbed pages you now hold in your hands.

MONDAY, OCTOBER 30, 7:50 A.M.

Scissors Cut Paper

Thomas died a month ago today.

WEDNESDAY, NOVEMBER 1, 9:01 P.M.

The Days of Burnout

With exams coming the week after Thanksgiving, teachers are loading us up with final papers and tests. Every other morning, I call my dad. Every Wednesday morning during my free period, I have my obligatory counseling session with Reverend Black and write poems in my head while he drones. Every day, I check my mailbox with no letter from Thomas's parents in it, but of course my letter to them is probably one of many requiring a response, and they can only handle so much. I imagine the Broughtons gathered around their dining-room table at Thanksgiving with no Thomas, his little brother Trenton trying too hard to keep things lively, trying too hard to keep his mother from crying in the cranberry sauce.

At night after study hall in the dorm common room, we gather at the TV, trying to find out, along with the rest of the American male population, when the NFL players' strike, which began in September, might end. On this Tuesday night, Glenn comes and sits on the arm of the sofa beside me. He pats me on the back like we're as normal as everyone else throwing popcorn and taking swigs from one another's Cokes. No one looks at us like we're criminals, and Auggie van Dorn asks if I know when the next Rolling Stones album is being released. (I don't.) When a Budweiser commercial with girls in bikinis comes on, Joe tells everybody to shut up and pay attention. "Like we need ears to understand *that*," Glenn says, pointing, and Auggie tells Joe that his sister hooked up with the Little Dipper at the St. Brigid mixer. "Gross," Andy says. "She looks just like Joe with long hair." It's true—she does—and we all have a big time with that one, except that I am thinking of her in the bushes with a kid who had to kiss the Buddha's stomach. Somehow, that makes me sad. And then Glenn whispers to me, "We need to talk." And that makes me nervous, so I stand and walk away, sad and nervous, when I should be walking away clearheaded and sleepy.

I go to my room, turn on the desk lamp, and wait. As usual, he enters without knocking. "We're doing the right thing. You know that, don't you?"

125

I say nothing.

"She knows, Stromm, but I need proof. If you'll steal her sweatshirt, then you won't mind sneaking into her apartment for a peek at her diary."

"I didn't steal her sweatshirt. And how do you know she keeps a diary?"

"All girls do."

"She's not a girl."

"Well, she's pretty darn close. She's only five years older than we are, if that. Plus, she's an English teacher, and English teachers love to write. It's in their blood." He looks at me hard. "You go in, and I'll stand guard."

"No. End of discussion."

"Aren't you dying to enter the inner sanctum?" He laughs. "Or have you entered it already?"

"Shut up."

"Mr. Mansfield believed me about her putting her hand on my knee. Because apparently someone told him that Miss Dovecott had been spotted sneaking into Wimberley Hall."

"Why would she sneak in? She's a teacher. She can walk in whenever she wants."

"At one o'clock in the morning?"

"Oh, come on."

"I told him she gave you her sweatshirt."

"At the river when I was soaking wet! She was just being nice!"

"She was being seductive."

"Is that your word, or Dean Mansfield's?"

"Mine. Dean Mansfield just took notes."

"He took notes? Jesus, Glenn, what else did you tell him?"

"I told him she shouldn't be here."

"She's a good teacher."

"She's an okay teacher. She's not better than Mr. Parkes."

"What does he have to do with anything?"

"I'm just saying."

"You are so paranoid, Glenn. Mr. Mansfield's not stupid. The whole Thomas thing, and Clay taking the fall. He knows better than anybody that where there's smoke, there's fire. You're going to get yourself in big trouble."

"Not if we win."

"Win what? What kind of game are you playing?"

"We," he says. "You are on *my* team. Remember?" He puts his hand on my shoulder.

"I'm not on anyone's team," I say, shaking him off. "You are out of control. Leave Miss Dovecott alone. If she really thought we were guilty of something, she would have turned us in a long time ago."

"Do you honestly believe that?"

"I do."

"Then you don't believe *me*. You have to believe me. You're my friend."

"I know I'm your friend."

"You're the smartest friend I have."

"I'm not that smart," I say. "I'm not as smart as you. I've never been on the Headmaster's List. You've been on it every single trimester."

"That's only because I know how to study. I wasn't stuck at some redneck junior high like you were." Glenn sighs. "I'm tired." And he sinks onto my bed.

"I'm tired, too," I say. "Maybe we should both just sleep until the end of the year."

"That's not what I mean. What if I— What if Clay—?"

"What?"

"Never mind."

"No, Glenn. Tell me."

He shakes his head. "What if Clay reneges on the deal?"

"He won't. Clay's back in Macon drinking beer every weekend and loving life. And even if he does, it will look like sour grapes. The investigation on the accident is closed. They're done with us."

"You and I have to look out for each other. My dad will literally die if I don't graduate from here."

"If you're so scared of your dad, then why don't you leave Miss Dovecott alone?"

All of a sudden, Glenn looks five years old. "I'm not scared of him. It's just that there are things he doesn't need to know. He thinks of Birch as some kind of Eden, and he wants it to be that way for me, too, and it isn't. It never will be."

The last thing I want to give Glenn is more ammunition, so I don't tell him what Miss Dovecott said at the mixer. She hasn't mentioned it since then, and I sure as hell don't want to bring it up, so this is what I say instead: "Even if you're right, that she knows more than she's telling, she's probably not going to write about it in some stupid diary. And she's not going to crawl into a hole just because some teenagers are harassing her."

He turns back into his pale-eyed self. "We are not dropping this, Stromm. You are going to sneak into her apartment and find out what she wrote in her diary about that day.

Don't give me any bullshit—you know you want to. You don't even have to steal it. Just open it up, read it, and get the heck out. We'll find out what her schedule is, and go from there. It's foolproof, easy as pie. In and out. Bang. Done."

"Bang," I say. "Just go ahead and shoot me."

The Dewey Decimal System

After Glenn leaves, I stand at the window, posted like a silent sentinel of Wimberley Hall, a mortal man fixed on woodland nightmares. I don't want to talk to Miss Dovecott about the accident, I want to talk with her about poems, but the truth of the matter is, Glenn is right about one thing: I want to know what else might be in that diary. I'm pretty sure Glenn is full of shit, but what if he isn't? Glenn's father the hero was in the same class at Birch as Dean Mansfield's younger brother. Dean Mansfield would certainly take that into consideration. Birch grads are loyal as hell to one another, life-long friends.

I grab my jacket and dash over to the library before the Lights-Out bell. This book I'm writing needs an editor. A pair of scissors. An honest voice. A decent plot. A climax. A moral. You name it, this book needs it. It is time to go back to the beginning, and for the beginning, I could choose an epigraph by Henry David Thoreau, which I would italicize if this were a real book:

I have always been regretting that I was not as wise as the day I was born. The intellect is a cleaver; it discerns and rifts its way into the secret of things.
—from "Where I Lived, and What I Lived For"

129

But where do I live, and what is it I'm living for? My physical self is sitting among Mr. Dewey's system, but this is not what Henry David meant. Knotholes in the brain: that is what he meant. The brain is like a tree, and the tree has roots so deep that you have no idea what it is that grounds you. I have my own selfish motives for going along with Glenn, and if I find out in the process that my English teacher is in love with me, then I'll come in my pants. But if I find out that she saw us drinking—all of us—then I'll have to follow through with The Plan. Which is to say: Get Her Gone.

She-Crab
(by Alex Stromm)

Claws red as fire,
stamped-on manicure.
Frailty, thy name

is Sally, what fisher-
men call you, all of you
one and the same.

Lose an arm in the tow,
shed the shell, breathe
farewell in the waves.

Behold the net, break
a leg in the chase,
what's left to pinch

but a fickle tide?
Callinectes, it mocks,
beautiful swimmer,

your siren song, your
genus. Bright pieces
wash up onshore.

Just like God, to shelter
the he-crab, blue claws
one with the water.

THURSDAY, NOVEMBER 2, 8:17 P.M.

The Part of The Plan That Golden Boy Keeps from Good, Solid Kid

I am already seated when Glenn struts into English class this morning wearing Miss Dovecott's sweatshirt. In less than a second, she knows that I'm a barbarian after all. She is looking straight at me, her eyes wild. Then she recovers, raises a fist in the air, Black Power–style, and says, "Go, Tigers," Princeton's mascot, and moves on to the lesson. She makes Glenn sit there for the rest of the class wearing it, something that is way too small for him. And she doesn't look at me again.

But here is an artist. He desires to paint you the dreamiest, shadiest, quietest, most enchanting bit of romantic landscape in all the valley.

FRIDAY, NOVEMBER 3, 8:36 P.M.

Moby-Dick

How many years did it take *Her*-man to write this novel anyway? I still can't get past the first chapter, its haunting sentences that won't let me escape. No ocean in sight, no wind or wing to carry me into the sky, far, far away.

Double-Dick

This is what I tell Glenn he is when we are in the bathroom down the hall from Miss Dovecott's classroom, after he has practically torn the sweatshirt off his body and handed it back to her on his way out the door. We stand at the urinals together, Glenn laughing at how I am so worked up over nothing. He knows, of course, that it is *something,* but there might be a person in the stall listening, so he plays it off like he's pulled some juvenile prank that will be forgotten in two hours. But I am really mad at him—really mad. I am not pretending when I tell him that over the past five weeks, he has officially turned into an asshole of the highest order.

"Then look at what that makes you," he says. "The Double-Dick's best friend."

The Barbarians

We do it under the cover of darkness. Our free periods don't match up with hers on Fridays, so Glenn makes an appointment with Miss Dovecott in her classroom fifteen minutes before the start of study hall to go over a rough draft of an upcoming essay, which means I have fifteen minutes to get in and out of her apartment. At 7:15, I check into the infirmary with a stomachache at the exact time when Nurse Patty administers allergy shots to the guys who require them. She directs me to one of the patient rooms down the hall right by the stairwell and tells me she'll be with me as soon as she can. I unzip my backpack and spread some books around on the cot. Then, with my flashlight tucked into my corduroys, I slip up the stairs to Miss Dovecott's apartment, which, in keeping with the Birch School community of trust, is unlocked.

I am more nervous than I am before a race, which is pretty damn nervous. Her living room is small, like a nook in a library. I run the flashlight up and down the books on a tall case, where I find three notebooks of hers from college, but no diary. I even check behind the large books, the dictionaries and anthologies: nothing.

Into the inner sanctum, which smells like mothballs. I check my watch for the time and then see her watch sitting on her bedside table. It looks alien without her slender wrist attached to it. I pick it up, and I'm cradling it in my palm when I hear the heavy front door of the infirmary bang once, then bang again. The Allergy Cats are heading to study hall. I pull open the rickety drawer of the table—a hair ribbon, a wadded-up tissue, a tiny silver box, and something that looks like a dead mouse that I am not about to touch. No diary, no journal, no secret letters of confession, nothing. With my flashlight, I check under the bed, under the mattress. When I check under the pillows on her double bed, which I would like to lie down on, I find a photograph of Miss Dovecott in profile with her arms around a tall young man bending down to gaze into her eyes. Something in my stomach flips, and I put the photo back where I found it, but upside down, like my stomach. I find my way back to the door into the stairwell with her watch still curled in my hand.

SATURDAY, NOVEMBER 4, 2:10 P.M.

Green Fields

One Saturday last March, Glenn and I walked down to the rock together. Clay was already there, with a senior from the wrestling team; Clay had told Glenn the day before to come on down because they were going to catch a buzz and jump. A nice guy, the wrestler; the heavyweight that year. He was always eating doughnuts, in and out of season; today was no exception. He had brought, from the canteen, a tray of the little powdered ones, which must have tasted like shit with the vodka.

I took a couple of sips and spit when no one was looking. I was scared of it in combination with the rock (much more scared than I was a month ago when the vodka was well at home in my bloodstream). I had been down to the river the day before to study the space between the rock and the water—thirty feet, maybe, like if you were standing on the roof of a three-story building. I had gotten very little sleep. I kept waking myself up from dreams of me falling, falling so deep into the water that I couldn't get back to the air.

We talked about how what we were doing was experimenting, just experimenting with fear. The heavyweight and I tried to laugh about how stupid it would sound to guys back at our old schools, like a club with an initiation, which was very third-grade. Glenn and Clay had jumped from it, stone-cold sober, the week before.

The wrestler told us about his twelve-year-old sister back in Kentucky. During spring break when he was home, she had a slumber party where the game of Truth or Dare turned into one big orgy. One of the girls had already developed breasts, and she took off her shirt. Some of the girls weren't even wearing bras yet, but they all took turns kissing the early bloomer. "How do you know all this?" I asked the guy. "Sharon told me," he said, simple as that, and I was never sure whether Sharon was his sister or the girl with the breasts.

I had heard before that girls practice kissing with one another so that they know what they're doing when a boy kisses them for real. But I kept my mouth shut about it because that day, on the way down to the rock, Glenn had tried to kiss me. He had tripped and fallen, and when I'd pulled him back up, he'd pushed his lips onto mine. Then he'd tried to play it off like he had just stumbled into my face.

DNA

Mr. Parkes preaches tonight because Reverend Black has laryngitis, and it is the best sermon I have ever heard. "There is God in all of us," he says. "God is programmed into our DNA, so He's there under our skin, biologically there, to connect us to a force larger than ourselves. It's what makes me feel not so alone in this world, as if inside of me is a seed, and if I nurture that seed, I can become my best far-reaching self." This is the first time that God has made sense to me, and I am writing it down so I won't forget it.

There is so much that I will forget. You think you'll remember every single thing about your life, but you won't. The morning after I entered the inner sanctum, a watchless Miss Dovecott had us make a list of images that were still in our heads from elementary school. It surprised me, how I couldn't recall the name of my second-grade teacher or what the cafeteria smelled like.

What I wrote down was a walk I took with my father one Christmas. It was snowing, a veil of white in front of us. My dad saw it first, grabbed my arm, and pointed at the buck, majestic, ten points at least. The buck was so still that everything around him seemed to be moving, even the trunks of the trees. I felt I'd been turned inside out, I felt the peak of happiness and the chasm of sadness. For the first time in my life, I sensed that I was growing older.

The other guys do not see what Miss Dovecott is doing for us. They do not see how she is working by degrees to get us back to a time when our minds were freer, more

136

connected to the world around us. More connected to what was programmed inside our DNA, just like Mr. Parkes said. I wonder if homosexuality is programmed there, too. Reverend Black says no, it's a choice. But if given the option, why would anyone choose that? I bet Mr. Parkes thinks what I think, that some guys are born that way, just like some guys are born with the gene for green eyes or stubby thumbs.

Before we are dismissed from chapel, Dean Mansfield takes the pulpit from Mr. Parkes for a special announcement. Miss Dovecott can't find her watch, which is of great sentimental value, so if anyone has seen it, please stay after for just a moment. Glenn, whose advisory group sits three rows in front of me, tilts his head ever so slightly in my direction.

MONDAY, NOVEMBER 6, 10:05 P.M.

Study Hall

No letter in my mailbox from Thomas's parents, but I do get a study hall summons. I failed a math test, which means that I'm assigned to proctored study hall until I pass the next one. Mandatory study for two and a half hours five nights a week in a room with forty other failures. Once a week, Miss Dovecott proctors. This week, it's Monday. Normally I'd be chomping at the bit for the chance to gaze at her for hours, but I am uneasy for reasons too obvious to state. I try to focus, biting my pencil as I work trigonometry problems. When I look up for a sneak peak, she is watching Neddy Sanderling, a new-boy goofball who has stuck two pencils up his nose, one for each nostril. Instead of telling him out loud to stop, she rises from her desk at the front of the room, and the senior sitting to Neddy's right notices, leans over, and punches him on the shoulder.

Then a guy sitting next to me—a football player named Aaron Botley—asks me in a whisper if he can borrow my math book, which I am using. I shake my head, and he asks me again. I shake my head more violently this time and turn away, at which point he grabs my notebook, without permission, without eye contact, and rips a blank sheet of paper out of it. I blink, but my shoulders do not move, and it is these seconds, this fleeting glimpse that Miss Dovecott could have so easily missed, that encapsulate who I am.

If I were a character in a novel, I would be half of a metaphor: in this world, some people are takers and some people allow themselves to be taken. The world, in the form of Aaron Botley, is stealing my innocence, piece by piece. What Miss Dovecott sees is the fact that I am a person who can be pushed beyond the normal limits of pushing.

But I could have stopped Aaron. *She* could have stopped Aaron. All she says to me after the bell rings to dismiss us is this: "I know you have a lot on your mind, Alex. That's what your poems are for, spaces to say those things."

I should have told her right then; I should have handed her my whole heart because she was the one who helped me to unfold it, to respect its knowledge and power—the part of the body that keeps every other part alive. I should have put my head in my hands and bawled like a baby, dropped to my knees and confessed that I'd signed on as a double agent, confessed that I'd stolen the watch, confessed, confessed, confessed. As I have done thousands of times, I swallow my gut reaction. I swallow who I am.

The Barbarians

Still no letter. When Glenn stops by my room before seated dinner tonight, he asks me for the fiftieth time where I've hidden the watch. I tell him yet again that I don't have it, just as I told him that I didn't find a diary in Miss Dovecott's apartment. He doesn't believe me. I don't care. If I were a teacher here and kept a diary, I would say, Screw the Birch School Community of Trust; I would keep it in the locked glove compartment of my car, not lying around for Barbarians to find.

THURSDAY, NOVEMBER 9, 7:20 P.M.

The Artists

In class, my pen is flying. I have to make it stop, slow down. I sense that she has assigned this in-class essay just for the artist in me. Miss Dovecott turns up the volume on the tape player, and I close my eyes, catching Mozart's bass line and following it as it pulses under the melody. She has told us that composers, like novelists, hide whole stories beneath the dazzle. When I open my eyes, I look around at my classmates' faces to see if I can pretend I've never seen them before, and I almost can. They are good-looking, all of them. A pimple here, a blackhead there, but no scar to be found, as if they've outgrown everything bad they've ever done.

Glenn hasn't written a word; he is staring at a blank sheet of paper. But, as Miss Dovecott has shown me, I work best when I jump right in and swim my way to an understanding. The curve of our necks as we bend forward to write strikes me as primordial, primeval. *This is the forest primeval:* what poem is that from? I have heard it before. Primeval. Prime evil.

I keep writing. I am the last one in the room. I can hear the next class waiting in the hall.

"Finished," I announce, smiling at Miss Dovecott, and in one single sweep, I scoop up my backpack and coat. As I reach my hand out across the desk to give her the essay, her fingers brush mine. She feels it, too, the shock, and our eyes brighten at the electricity. Skin holds a knowledge all its own. I am not exactly sure what grace is, but I think this moment might be something very close to it.

But moments of grace are fleeting. Glenn stops by my room on his way to football practice to tell me that Miss Dovecott assigned us the in-class essay to try to ferret out the guy who stole her watch. "She's sneaky," he says. "She'll read into those things like there's no tomorrow. And you know what, Stromm? For her there might not be. Don't forget The Plan."

"Get the f^ck out of my room," I say, and he does.

(I am leaving space here to copy my response to the prompt Miss Dovecott gave us, once I get it back from her.)

My Response

I'm not going to write about the Honor Code at this school. We all know what that is; it has been drummed into our heads since before we even arrived here. I'm going to write about what I think honor really is, which is something this school never discusses.

Honor is truth. Truth has many meanings, but it first means that you have to be true to yourself. It is hard to be true to yourself because it is hard to be yourself. I have a feeling it's going to be one of those things that I struggle with all my life, like religion. I bet some people go through their whole lives living someone else's life. It's hard to put into words what I'm trying to say, but if it takes a lifetime to form your identity and arrive at the truth of who you are, then haven't you, in some sense, been living a lie?

How do you ever know who you really are, when your society and world teach you to hide? You hide things every day, most of all your feelings, but you are conditioned to, especially if you are a boy. I remember the day when you asked us to write about the concealing paint that we wore at pep rallies that liberated us into our savagery. Well, this reminds me of that because we are taught to wear masks that hide our true selves, which have the capacity for evil.

It's the question philosophers have debated for centuries: is man basically good or basically evil? If we really want to be honest with ourselves—that is to say, if we really want to be honorable—then the truth here is that we all have a little God inside of us—God did make us in His image, like the Bible says—but we also have evil, a little Satan inside of us, too. And that is a scary thought. I've done some bad things in my life, some very bad things, and the worst one is the one I think you know, which I have never admitted to anyone, and hardly even to myself: my friend was unconscious in the river while I was goofing around. Valuable seconds were wasted—I wasted valuable seconds, first in the water and then when I was running. But I got scared, I panicked. I crouched at the base of a tree for a moment or two to get a grip on myself. Maybe my friend was still alive then, maybe he was. If he was, then it was no one's fault but mine that he died.

What's hard for me is that a few people in this world, including you and my dad, think I'm this decent guy. But I have dark places inside of me. I have seen things that I can never describe, things so black that the person I was before has disappeared. If I'm to live an honest life, then I'm going to have to acknowledge that the darkest holes in my heart and my soul have truth to them, too. (I'm running out of time here, and I know this is very disorganized, so it's okay if I don't get a good grade because it's not a good piece of writing. But at least it's honest, and it's what I really do think.)

Here is an artist. He desires to paint the dreamiest, shadiest, quietest, most enchanting bit of romantic landscape in all the valley. Yes, this is how I see it play out: like a knight, in defense of Miss Dovecott, I will beat up Glenn for the things he is doing to her; I will finally have it out with him, and the school will have to dismiss me for "conduct unbecoming of a Birch student," but everyone will know that it was actually honorable behavior, the age-old code of chivalry. Then, Miss Dovecott will be so grateful and so much in love with me that she will welcome me into her life with open arms, filling me with her inspiration so that I don't waste away in public high school. My dad will find a good woman, too—we'll double-date in Asheville, going to concerts and foreign films and poetry readings—and he will eventually get over the disgrace of my dismissal.

Bad Monkey

And she will understand why I snuck into the inner sanctum, looking for proof. And she will understand why I took her watch, which I slide onto my wrist every night before I go to bed. I lie on my back, let everything go quiet, and breathe in rhythm with the ticking. With her watch on my skin, it's like she's touching me, not me touching myself. In the mornings before I take a shower, I tuck the watch into the stuffing of my pillow, where I've cut a slit in the lining just wide enough for my fingers.

FRIDAY, NOVEMBER 10, 7:15 P.M.

Field Trip

When Miss Dovecott walks into her classroom, I can hardly look at her without a sweet pain tightening my stomach, without a surge of adrenaline through my blood. Has she read our essays yet? She doesn't hand them back first thing as she usually does; instead, she reads us the announcements. Today is Bailey Richards's birthday, and he runs with it.

"Please, Miss Dovecott, don't give us a quiz," he says. "This is definitely not a quiz day."

"Yeah," says Joe Bonnin. "That stuff we had to read last night was impossible."

"Well, tell me what you understood, and if you can do that, we'll forgo the quiz."

"Forgo?" asks Bailey. "Does that mean that we're having one at the end of the period?"

"Alex," says Joe, "you tell her."

"Joe," says Miss Dovecott, "I asked you."

After Joe flips his notebook open, he says, "I think I might have left the handout in my room."

"Okay, then. Just tell me what you remember."

Bailey and a couple of other guys start laughing because we all know that even if he did do the work, he won't remember. Like a bunch of other Birch students, Joe's a legacy, which means he can be as dumb as he wants.

"Well," he says, "that David Henry Through guy—"

"Henry David Thoreau."

"Whoever. He liked the woods. He went there to live inside his bones, or something like that. Something about bones. That's part of what I didn't understand."

"Marrow," says Jovan Davis. "Not bones."

Miss Dovecott nods. "Go ahead, Joe."

As Joe flounders to make sense of the excerpt from *Walden,* I look around the room. The light in our eyes there at the start of class is dimming.

"Henry said to eat only one meal a day," Joe says. "To keep things simple. I don't get it, though, because it seems like that would be more complicated because you'd be hungry all the time."

Miss Dovecott walks over to the light switch and flips it off. The guys who had planned to tuck it in for the period lift their heads. "Without saying a word, I want you to stand up, put on your coats, and follow me. Then we're going to come back and talk through the passage, sentence by sentence."

In silence we follow her through the front door, across the quad, and up the hill to the edge of the woods. Fog lies low,

144

turns the trees edging the campus into undefined smudges like smeared pencil marks.

"Field trip!" Joe shouts, but Miss Dovecott shushes him by putting a finger to her lips.

We are standing on the ridge when the geese fly over, dozens, so many that we can hear the flapping of their wings. Because of the fog, we can't see them. We listen for long minutes, letting our ears become our eyes. I close my eyes, feeling the moist air on my skin, pretending it's Haley's breath panting up and down my body. I open my eyes only when it's time to follow the teacher down the hill.

Back at our desks, Miss Dovecott reads us the last paragraph of "Where I Lived, and What I Lived For." I glance at Glenn for the first time all day, and under these lights, his face looks gray. Thoreau's sentences buzz around me, through me, as I hear the wings once more over my head. And then Miss Dovecott tells us that Thoreau, who vowed to rough it on the edge of a pond for a year, left Walden every now and then to take his dirty clothes home for his mom to wash. F^ck Thoreau. Thoreau is a pussy of the highest order. At the very least, he is a poser just like the rest of us.

Grilled Cheese

Glenn and I and a bunch of other guys sit in the dining hall savoring our hour of freedom before another afternoon of classes. Some guys eat fast so they can cram for a test or squeeze in a nap or play Pac-Man on the one machine downstairs. There is a time limit on the machine because otherwise, some nerds would never stop playing. Anyway, the other guys get up to go all at once, which leaves me and Glenn there alone at the table. We realize it at the exact same time that we're eating what was Thomas's favorite lunch. Glenn's eyes shimmer for a minute, then glaze over, but not before he smiles the saddest smile I've ever seen, which I take as some kind of an acknowledgment. Of what, I'm not sure.

He looks around to make sure no one is listening. No one is. He tells me that when Miss Dovecott called him in for a conference on his honor essay, she told him his essay needed work, that it was vague, lacking in depth and development, and she asked him to rewrite it. He tells me he thought he saw Mr. Henley out in the hall, watching them through the window.

And just then, out of nowhere, Mr. Henley appears at our lunch table and pats Glenn on the back. "How's that rewrite coming along?" he asks with a smile. Glenn and I smile along.

"Mr. Stromm, I understand that you have decided to enter a national essay contest. Good for you. And, Mr. Stromm, once you find fame and fortune, don't forget us little people. Submit some of your poems to *Bark* (*Bark* being the school's art and literary magazine). I hear you're quite a talent."

"Yes, sir," I say. "I mean, that's nice of you to say. I'll do my best." When I turn back to Glenn to tell him he's an asshole, to tell him once and for all that, due to lack of evidence, I refuse to execute the last play of The Plan, he has disappeared.

Mailbox

Still nothing from the Broughtons. A postcard from my dad in Acadia National Park, where it is snowing. As I am standing there reading it, I hear Reverend Black's twangy voice down the hall, coming closer, and I duck outside. I want to cry the guilt out of my body, it is drowning me. Oh, Dad, how will I look you in the eye without your knowing that all I am doing these days is fighting for air?

And I only am escaped alone to tell thee. (from the first chapter of *Moby-Dick* and the book of Job)

SATURDAY, NOVEMBER 11, 4:00 P.M.

I borrow words from *Her*-man. *Her*-man borrows words from God. Someday someone might borrow words from me. I want to be a writer when I grow up, maybe a poet. Poetry is a language unto itself, where words carry more than their weight, where white space on the page is profound silence. Poetry is a way of seeing the world with your feelings. Life is not meant to be taken so literally, and in my case, that is a huge relief.

Final Pep Rally

How do I begin to describe how the Birch School alums, especially the ones who are freshmen in college, act when they return for homecoming with something to prove? Some of them travel hundreds of miles for Friday night's event, but when they get here, they walk around in their L.L.Bean moccasins and rag wool sweaters, gripping tightly to plastic cups emblazoned with the name of a socially acceptable university. (The guys who go to loser schools never advertise it.) The alums get drunker and drunker, and inevitably one of them will take a piss in the middle of the quad or streak through his old dorm just because he can. At least one of them will end up in a dorm bathroom, where he'll waste the night praying to the porcelain god. This is the one time a year when the school actually hires a security guard.

Before the lighting of the bonfire, the alumni gather behind us, and if they're sober or gentlemanly enough, they'll speak to us. Some of the theater majors or the Campus Crusaders for Christ hang out with the faculty. But wherever they are, and whoever they're with, they cheer as the lit torches come hurtling through the air onto the two-story tower of branches. Everyone cheers in the heat of the moment.

This year, the cheers melt into shouts of Miss Dovecott's name, her first name. "Hey-LEE!" Clap, clap. "Hey-LEE!" Clap, clap. Before she can run from where she stands with Mr. Parkes and the younger members of the faculty, Ted Ferenhardt touches her shoulder and escorts her to the platform.

The cheer masters always tap a teacher to lead the charge, but this is the first time they've tapped a female teacher. No one knows how this is going to go, but the whole teeming mass is whooping a war cry, "Whoo-hoo! Whoo-hoo!" while Miss Dovecott looks like Wendy about to walk the plank of the *Jolly Roger*. Everybody, even the alums, is cheering for her.

A cheer master in a mask helps her onto the platform. "Red hot!" he shouts into her face and jumps up and down. He grabs her hands so that she has to jump with him. "Higher!"

he shouts at her. "Faster!" She jumps up and down like a maniac, hair flying out of her ponytail. Then he shouts to the crowd. "Red hot! Let's hear it for Miss Dovecott! Red hot, red hot! Let's hear it for Miss Dovecott!"

Miss Dovecott's face burns as she becomes a rhyme. Her only way out is to join in, become one of us. So she does. In a zombie voice she leads the charge: "Our team is red hot, our team is red hot! Our team is r-e-d—red—h-o-t—hot! Once we start, we can't be stopped. Red! Red hot!" She stumbles over the monosyllables, but it doesn't matter what the words are, only the loudness of them.

Miss Dovecott may have expected the cheers to turn to mocking laughter, but they do not. The stage and its rituals are sacred. As her name fades, Ted Ferenhardt takes front and center and shouts, "Let's hear it for Miss Dovecott, who is, whoo-hoo, red hot!" He will rack up a few demerits for that, but he will also get pats on the back for at least a week, and in a way, it's payback for the gingerbread incident, so it's worth it. Ted grins like a crazy man while Miss Dovecott looks at her feet. A football player in a black hood escorts her down, and I wonder if she recognizes Glenn Everson's pale, unreadable eyes as they flatline into her own.

It's the same stare he gives me later that night in my room as I tell him the truth. "I don't want to hurt Miss Dovecott. And she doesn't deserve to get kicked out of here because of a lie. No one does."

"It won't be a lie, not if you make it happen the right way."

"Nothing is going to happen."

"Stromm, you stole her watch. You know it, and I know it, and if you don't go through with this, then I'll tell Miss Dovecott you did it."

"You wouldn't," I say, meaning it.

"Watch me. Pun intended."

"That's blackmail. Pun intended. 'Black,' as in 'dark.' 'Male,' as in 'you and me.' And I can rat you out, too."

"For what?"

"For drinking vodka at the river."

"If I go down for that, so will you," Glenn says. "Besides, who are they going to believe—a thief or a Golden Boy?"

"You're not so golden," I say. "There are other things I could blackmail you for, but I'm not that kind of guy."

"Like what?"

I give him my own stare, a dark one. "What Thomas told me right before he died."

Hide-and-Seek

I do not go to the final football game of the season on Saturday afternoon. I could not care less whether we win or lose or even how we play the game. Football is a dirty sport, unlike cross-country, which is pure. In running, you have a clear winner and loser, no referees with their subjectivity, no masks or pads to hide behind. You are in competition with other runners from other teams, of course, but mainly, you are in competition with yourself, and that makes you try all the harder because if you can beat yourself, you can beat anything.

So I go for a run with Miss Dovecott's watch tucked inside my shorts, using it to take note of my progress. I am out

151

to conquer my best time, which is an 18:20. But because of the extra weight in my brain, I end up running the 3.1-mile course in a flat 19. Not a time that would earn a place in a meet or a pat on the back from Mr. Wellfleet.

Back in my library carrel, I open my journal to a blank page. It scares me, all of that white, so I take my pen in my right hand, flatten my left hand to the paper, and draw an outline around it, the way you did when you were a kid. Sometimes you made a turkey out of it for Thanksgiving, coloring the fingers in with reds and yellows, adding an eye and a wattle to the thumb. I do not make a turkey, even though Thanksgiving break is a week away. I draw lines across the palm, life lines, they're called. Have you ever noticed how much they look like rivers and streams, creeks and tributaries? Water hiding out in our own hands. Water, water, everywhere, but not a drop to drink. I rip the drawing out of my journal and tear it into tiny pieces, which I let fall, a pathetic imitation of rain, into a library trash can.

MONDAY, NOVEMBER 13, 7:22 A.M.

The Artists

After dinner and chapel, I knock on the door of Miss Dovecott's classroom. She is there on a Sunday night, grading papers, head bowed. She looks like she's praying. With her, it's serious business; with some other teachers, not so much. You see them hurrying through tests at the breakfast table or even at basketball games. Their red pens move across the page while their eyes move across the court. Sometimes in class, when you're going over a quiz or test, you'll catch a teacher's mistake, and usually the teacher is pretty nice about giving you the points back. Some of them even tell you that if they make a mistake in your favor not to call their attention to it.

She waves me in. "I'm glad you're here," she says. "I read your honor essay."

"Oh," I say. "That."

"Listen, Alex. Is there anything else you'd like to tell me about that day?" She gestures for me to sit in one of the nearby desks, and I do, avoiding Thomas's old desk.

"What do you mean?"

"Well, you appear to have run out of time in your essay. I thought perhaps there was more you would have liked to put down on paper."

I think about my journal-novel and almost smile; the whole thing, those strings and strings of words, seems so absurd. "You were there, too," I say. "It was confusing."

"What was?"

I point to my brain. "What was going on up here as compared to what was happening on the ground. You know me, Miss Dovecott. I don't always lead with my head."

"That's what makes you such a good poet."

"Speaking of that," I say, "I was . . . Well, I was wondering. Do you think we could get together every now and then and read over my poems? Because I know they could be better. You could help me make them better. Mr. Henley has encouraged me to submit some to *Bark,* and I want to send in my best."

She says it would be a *pleasure.* She suggests that we set up a weekly appointment; one thing every good writer needs to succeed, she tells me, is discipline, and a weekly meeting would keep me productive and focused.

"That would be great," I say, and thank her.

"Did you just change the subject on purpose?"

I play dumb, something I'm pretty good at. "How did I change the subject?"

She looks at me, hard. "Well, you know where my sign-up sheet is." She points to the wall. "And if there's more you want to tell me, you know where to find me."

I walk over to the sign-up sheet. "These conferences are during your free periods, right?" I take a breath. "It'd be more convenient for me—that is, if it's okay with you—to meet after dinner, when I have more time. You're in your classroom sometimes after dinner anyway. I know that's a lot to ask. . . ."

"Not for you, Alex," she says. "Not for you."

"How about if we meet this Thursday, then?"

"Okay."

"In your apartment?"

"No, Alex. We'll meet here."

(You can't blame a guy for trying.)

I go, out of her classroom, out the front door of Sellers Hall. When I reach my room, I lock my door, which, in the Birch School spirit of trust, we aren't supposed to do except when we leave for vacation, and I grab my purple pen. What pours out of it that night is purest poetry, as you can see.

Goldilocks
by Alex Stromm (1966–)

She's like a child without a corner;
too small behind the teacher's desk,
too short beside the chalk tray, too thin
to carry the books stacked on the shelf.

154

But she is ready to be there, in her heart;
the words that drop from her mouth
rise again, pearl balloons, and her voice
is gentle and will not pop them.

It just isn't a place for soft vowels.
When she tries to fit, she snags her dress,
scrapes her knee, breaks her finger in the lock.
No baby bear to befriend—

the babies are all gone, or grown.
There is no world to make her own.

If you are a girl, Birch's five hundred acres are a paradise. Most faculty daughters are sent away to boarding school once they hit puberty. I swear I never have—because if my dad ever found out, he would kill me—but most of my class-mates talk about which faculty daughter they'd most like to f^ck. I've seen the way the older girls, the ones who aren't sent away and go to the public school, look at Glenn. He doesn't look back. Though he could say to all of them, "Meet me in the boxwoods behind the library at midnight," and every single one of them would, I guarantee it.

Double O Seven

Even before I knock on the door of Miss Dovecott's class-room Monday night after dinner, I feel like a criminal, like an honest-to-God double agent. I am here on too many missions.

"Alex," she says, "I didn't expect you until Thursday."

"I have poems," I say.

"I have work," she says, pointing to her stack of essays.

"I'm kind of eager for you to read this one," I say. "Just one. I won't keep you long."

"Well, let's have a look, then." She smiles, waving me into the room.

I pull the folder of poems out of my backpack, and she comes out from behind her desk.

"You sit there," she says, pointing, "and I'll sit across from you. The way this will work best, I think, is if you read the poem out loud, without my looking at it, and then I'll read it out loud to you so you can hear your words in someone else's voice. And then we'll talk through it."

Although I want her next to me, not across from me, I begin. "This first poem is called 'Goldilocks.'" And I read. When I finish, I can hear the overhead fluorescent lights buzzing.

"It's a sonnet," she says.

"Well, a loose one."

"It's about me," she says.

"It's a tribute."

156

"No one has ever written a poem about me before," she says, her face turning red.

"Well, it's about time," I say as I watch the blush creep all the way to her hairline. "Now, it's your turn." I hand her the sheet of paper.

After hearing the poem in her voice, I want to make the whole thing rhyme. Miss Dovecott agrees: it will give the poem more tension, she says, the rhymes versus the subject not being able to fit.

"But the rhymes, in a way, allow her to fit," I say, looking at her.

"Maybe you're right, Alex." She closes her mouth, opens it to speak, closes it again. She reaches for her watch, forgetting it's not there, and grabs on to her wrist.

And in that moment I realize that if Thomas hadn't died, she would never have taken an interest in me. I would have been just another polite student with nothing important to say, a kid yet to come into his own. I would have never written a poem other than the ones I was required to write.

"Alex," she says. "How do I say this?"

"Say what?" I hold my breath, thinking, This is it, here it comes, she is going to tell me she loves me. But that is not what she says.

She says, "I'm afraid that after you leave this class, you'll stop writing. Life will get in the way, it will move too fast, and you won't make time for these." She lifts the poem up, holding it out to me. "Promise me that, whatever happens, you'll keep writing."

"I promise," I say.

157

"And I promise that you will always have at least one faithful reader. But now I've got miles to go before I sleep, so I'll see you Thursday with a new poem." She walks to the door while I gather my things, and she holds it open for me.

I run straight out into the night, running fast, as if pulled by the moon hanging over the campus like an examiner's bulb. The stars fuzz in my eyes, now blurry with cold, and in the distance a dog barks. I wonder if dogs ever feel as lonely as people. After my mom left, Freud, our golden retriever, kept climbing at night onto her side of the bed even though he had never slept there before, and when my dad finally got around to buying Freud his own special cushion, which Freud refused, I dragged him into my bed and fell asleep listening to his heart beat.

Bed, bed: where I need to be, the place I know best, my home away from home. But almost as soon as I close the door to my room and curl into the fetal position, Glenn walks in.

"I'm sick," I tell him.

"Alex," he says. He hardly ever calls me Alex. I sit up. "Alex," he says again, "do you think that Thomas is looking down at us right now?"

And with that, Glenn sounds like the old Glenn, the one I used to like, the one I became friends with. He looks like the old Glenn, too, his pale eyes clear with light, not murky with confusion. "Sometimes I think that," I say.

"Poet-boys think that all the time, I bet."

"Yeah," I say. "Pretty much."

"I think it all the time, too. And I'm a math guy."

"Math is all right."

"You hate math."

"Yeah, I know, but just because I hate it doesn't mean it isn't worthwhile."

"Hey," says Glenn, "maybe we should do something for Thomas, like a tribute or something."

"You mean like the fountain?"

"No, not anything stupid, completely insensitive, totally morbid, not to mention tasteless. Something real. Something we know Thomas would appreciate."

I think for a minute. "Well, how about a plaque? Like those ones in the chapel of the guys who died in the wars."

"I don't think it should hang in the chapel. I'd feel like a hypocrite."

"How about in Miss Dovecott's classroom, then, or someone else's? We could put it on the wall near his desk. Or *on* his desk."

"Thomas didn't really like school," says Glenn. "He liked girls and fishing and girls and grilled cheese sandwiches and girls. So where does that leave us?"

"Girls."

"Speaking of girls"—he pauses dramatically—"how's Haley?"

"Fine."

"How did she like your honor essay?"

"She gave me a B-plus. There were some grammatical errors."

I do not tell him I confessed; I do not tell him that I stopped running for a few precious minutes and hid by the tree with the knothole.

"If you can find out how much she knows, then we can lay everything to rest," Glenn says. "I mean it. Everything. We can get back to the way we were before all of this happened."

"That's impossible."

"So forget The Plan—fine. With a little luck, she'll get her own self booted. Giving boys her clothes, touching them where she shouldn't—it'll happen in its own good time. I'm talking about putting the whole Thomas thing behind us so that we can move forward with our lives. You want that, don't you?"

"Yeah."

"And Thomas would want that for us. Seriously, Stromm, think about the tribute. We owe him. And think about doing your duty as a man of your word. You owe that to yourself." He walks to the door and turns back. "She's using you. You realize that, don't you?"

The idea falls on my heart like an anchor.

"She's turning you into a poet to make herself look good. She's the sculptor; you're clay. If she succeeds with you, then it's a mark in her favor. The administration's suspicious."

"Thanks to you."

"She needs to prove she's valuable here. You're her ticket."

"She doesn't need me. She's helped lots of guys."

"But you're her pet."

"I'm not a dog, Glenn. And she's not my master."

"No," he says with a big smile. "I am. I am the captain of this ship, and you are my first mate, my right-hand man." Then he closes the door so quietly behind him that I have to look to make sure he is really gone.

I slump back to my pillow with thoughts orbiting my

brain like planets, worlds unto themselves. What if Miss Dovecott *is* using me and my poems to slip inside the Old Boy Network that creeps across the ground here like ivy, using me and my poems to get to the heart of her suspicions? What made her suspicious in the first place? My essay? The scattered ideas of an unreliable narrator? I pull the essay out of my English folder, read it over again. I don't see anything there that an innocent boy wouldn't write, too, under the circumstances. I feel old; I feel doomed. I think about how Thomas will soon be one of the dead boys trapped in the school's musty yearbooks. And I only am escaped alone to tell the tale—I only. I conjure Miss Dovecott's voice reciting my poems, the clip-clop of the lines carried in her voice, her rocking voice, which is the rocking of the water, which is the rocking of my body as I lay me down to sleep.

The great floodgates of the wonder-world swung open.

FRIDAY, NOVEMBER 17, 7:03 A.M.

Captain Ahab has an obsession that clouds his judgment. To believe that he has the power to bring down a whale, to believe that he can battle what God made, and win: this is his hubris, his tragic flaw. Melville was right to title his masterpiece with the obsession itself because it looms, ghostlike, over every nautical mile.

On Wednesday I find the flyer in my English notebook tucked behind my explication of Dickinson's "I Felt a Funeral, in My Brain." The deadline for the contest I told Miss Dovecott I'd enter was Tuesday. I throw the flyer away in a library trash can. There are a million guys like me out there, being encouraged by their teachers; there is no way I would have won a thing. The judges would have laughed all over my paper, saying, "Who does he think he is?"

My thoughts precisely: who does he think he is? Take your pick: reader, writer, son, lifeguard, lover of water, lover

162

of Haley (in his dreams), dreamer, nephew, cousin, friend, student, teammate, Bulldog, hater of vodka and hypocrites, hypocrite, janitor, Tarheel fan, caretaker (of Freud). He is Is Male, boy among boys at a school in 1982, and he'll leave it as others have left it, as others will leave it, boys stepping into who they are without ever having known who they were. Even with words of identification beside his photograph in the yearbook, he will go down, down in history, a drop in the bottomless bucket of time.

ALEXANDER NO MIDDLE NAME STROMM
Black Mountain, North Carolina

(INSERT PHOTO HERE)

They shall mount up with wings as eagles; they shall run, and not be weary.
—ISAIAH 40:31

It is better to fail in originality than to succeed in imitation. —MELVILLE

You can't always get what you want.
—THE ROLLING STONES

Ball Park franks: plump when you cook 'em. —A. H.

All-State Cross-Country, '83; All-Conference Cross-Country, '82, '83; Poetry Editor, *Bark*, '83–'84; Headmaster's List, '83–'84

Alexander No Middle Name Stromm

At our designated poetry-meeting time on Thursday night, I knock on Miss Dovecott's classroom door. I have my poems,

I have my heart beating faster than it does after I've finished a race. I have never been so aware of this organ of mine that looks like a fist, clenched and bloody. Whoever it was who first equated hearts with valentines was way off. The heart is a weapon.

She is ready for me. She gestures toward the empty desk, the one that no one sits in anymore. "Have a seat."

When she turns to get the chair from behind her desk, I sit in the desk nearest the empty one. She either doesn't notice or chooses not to comment as she pulls her chair up so that she faces me. "I take it you sent your essay in to the contest," she says, smiling. "I sent in my part last week."

"Actually, Miss Dovecott, I didn't. I'm sorry you spent time recommending me when I didn't even send anything in."

"Why?"

"I've got a lot on my mind these days," I tell her, "and sometimes I can't make it do what I want it to do." I pause. "Can I ask you a question first that has nothing to do with writing?"

"I'm not sure I'll be able to answer it, but you may ask it."

I stare at the clock on the wall. "When Thomas died. You were there. But maybe you were there before that. I mean, a few minutes earlier? Were you?"

"I didn't see you run and then stop running, like you said in your honor essay, if that's what you mean."

"Well, I'm glad you didn't see that, but, no, that's not what I mean."

She looks at me with her deep eyes. "You want to know everything I saw."

164

"Yes."

She hesitates. And that's when I know that Glenn is right—there *is* more to the story. I nod, wiping my palms on my corduroys, and stare at her pearls, how the right side of her necklace holds the light. Half of everything blooms white.

"I'll tell you," she says, "if you tell me first what it is you are afraid I saw."

"Miss Dovecott, that's not fair."

"Sure it is. I already know there's more to the story, Alex. I've read between the lines, and I'm usually pretty good at that."

"If I tell you, can we keep it just between us?"

"That depends," she says.

"On what?"

"On how much of it actually *is* just between us."

"You know that it's not," I say.

"Well, then, it's your choice, Alex. Don't tell me if you feel the need to protect someone other than yourself. But if you do choose to tell me, I ask that it be the truth."

I take a deep breath, thinking, If I go down with the ship, I go down with the ship. "I was drinking vodka, too. Clay told Mr. Armstrong I wasn't, but I was. Maybe if I hadn't been, I would have been able to stop Thomas. He was so drunk, there was no way we'd ever get him back up the hill; someone would see him, someone would know, and we'd all be sent home. When he dove from the rock, he could hardly stand up straight. We thought swimming would sober him up. We—I—should never have let him do it."

She touches her wrist where her watch used to be, her fingers lost without time to hold on to.

165

"So," I ask, "are you going to tell on me?"

"As hard as it might be for you to believe, it wasn't that long ago that I was seventeen. To be honest with you, a part of me doesn't care about the vodka."

"Then what do you care about?"

"You."

I hold my breath.

"Trust me—it's not going to do anyone any good for me to blow the whistle now on the drinking. At the time, Dean Mansfield asked me if I saw any evidence of alcohol or drugs, or smelled any, and I didn't. That's the truth."

I exhale, remembering Glenn's licorice gum.

"You have a gift, Alex. You have no idea how gifted you are. And I shouldn't tell you that because I'm afraid it will go to your head, and then you'll grow complacent and lazy. If you go back to public school, I'm afraid you'll become your lesser self."

I pull my folder of poems to my stomach. "Don't you think I deserve to be kicked out?"

"By the letter of the law, yes."

"But you don't want me to go."

"No, I don't want you to go." She takes a deep breath. "You remind me of someone, a boy in my third-grade class who told me that he had a secret set of wings growing on the inside of his shoulder blades and that one day the wings would push through the skin and lift him into the sky. This is hard to explain, but there is something about you, Alex, that makes me want to run to the library and learn everything there is to learn about birds."

I gaze at my feet, which look as if they want to walk away from my body.

"You don't need me to write, Alex. You have what you need right here." She taps my head, and I look up.

"I thought it was here," I say, touching my heart. "I thought the poems were here."

"Maybe they are. What do I know?"

"But you're the teacher."

"Sometimes, Alex, I'm the student." She rises, and I rise with her.

"In a way, I wish you *would* tell on me," I say. "It might make me feel better, to have it all out in the open. But I don't want Glenn to get in trouble because of me."

"For what?" She jumps on it. "What did he do?"

"Well, he was drinking, too."

"Yes?"

"And he—"

"What, Alex? What do you know?"

"What do *you* know?"

"Do you understand, Alex, that I trust you?"

"Yes," I say.

"All I know is that I have my doubts about Glenn. And I suspect you do, too."

Panic shoots up my spine, and I try to read her face. "What do you mean?"

"I was almost at the end of the trail when I heard the shouts, so it took me a few minutes to get back to where you all were, but when I got there, Glenn was bent over Thomas. He was holding his hand over Thomas's face."

"To feel if he was breathing—"

"I don't know, Alex." She slows down her words. "Glenn was crying. He was holding his hand on Thomas's face, and he was crying."

"Because Thomas was dead."

Miss Dovecott looks at me with her Emily Dickinson eyes, and the great floodgates of the wonder-world swing open.

"You're going to blow the whistle," I say.

"How can I do that when I'm not sure of what I saw? All this time, I've wondered. All this time, I've been watching Glenn, thinking he might somehow reveal it to me. Or maybe he told you." She pauses. "I thought you might know."

Something flares inside my chest, and I turn away, the ache of truth alive in my throat. She *is* using me.

"Do you know, Alex?"

"No," I say, choking out the word.

"Glenn never talked to you about it?"

I shake my head.

"Is there a chance you might have even seen it yourself? What I saw?"

"It was too far away from where I was hiding."

"But in your essay, you wrote that you thought Thomas might have still been alive. You had a *feeling*, at least, even if you couldn't see it. Right?"

I shrug. "Maybe."

"Did Glenn have any reason, any reason in the world, to hurt Thomas?"

I run my hand along the edge of my folder of poems, praying she'll read between the lines so that I don't have to tell her.

"Glenn is hiding something," she says. "Something big."

I open the folder, refusing to look at her.

"Can you tell me what it might be? Alex?"

"I can't tell you because it might not be the truth."

"Why is that?"

"Because it's rumor, not fact. And you know how boarding schools are: Rumor Central."

I look at her now, thinking she'll remember our conversation at the mixer and put it all together. But the pieces of her puzzle are different than the pieces of my puzzle.

"Has it not ever occurred to you, Alex, that Glenn might have orchestrated the whole thing? That whole day at the river. Getting Thomas so drunk that he couldn't stand up straight. The jumping from the rock. Please answer my question. To your knowledge—to your intellectual *and* emotional knowledge—did Glenn have any reason to want Thomas out of the picture?"

I want to pick up the words that have fallen out of her mouth and hide them away somewhere dark, somewhere deep. My head is so heavy that it feels like a boulder, but I hold it up long enough to say what I have to say. "No, ma'am." The words come out in a whisper, and I watch the hope that was lingering in her eyes a moment ago slip quietly away.

"You're sure about that. Absolutely sure."

"Yes, ma'am."

169

"Alex?"

I do not respond because I might throw up all over my poems.

"Alex. Whatever happens from this point, there will be a silver lining—there is always a silver lining. You will learn from this. We all will. And the next time you're confronted with a choice, maybe you'll make the right one."

I lift my head slightly. "I don't know what you mean." But I know exactly what she means. There is so much doubt in her face—doubt in me, doubt in herself, doubt in the whole world, probably.

"It's time for you to leave," she says, standing. "Go, do your homework for tomorrow."

"What about the poems?" I stand, too, my knees shaking, and hold out my folder.

"The poems can wait. I'll see you in the morning, Alex." She shows me to the door.

Out in the night, under the pinprick stars, my life begins to rearrange itself under a different light.

The Drama's Done. Why then here does any one step forth? —Because one did survive the wreck.

SATURDAY, NOVEMBER 18, 7:32 A.M.

Hide-and-Seek

Is Male is running out of paper; Is Male is running out of driftwood. Although Is Male has not yet gone down with the ship, he can only hold on for so long. But Truth, it will survive: it treads water for as long as it needs to until it spies land, rides in with the tide, and plants its roots in the soil.

Behind *Moby-Dick,* Is Male will hide his no-longer-blank pages until the time is right. Who cares about white whales in this day and age? No one will find Is Male here with his title-less book. The title is the writer's stamp of approval, and Is Male does not approve. Truth fights for air, and when it finds air, Is Male the Liar is going down.

Masterpiece, Timepiece

After I stop shaking, after I go to the library and write and put my journal back in its hiding place, I find Glenn in his room. I have Clay's Bible with me, the one he left behind, and when I ask Glenn to place his right hand on it, he does not argue.

"I swear to God that I put my hand on Thomas's face to see if I could feel breath on my palm," Glenn says calmly. "I felt nothing because Thomas was dead." He hands the Bible back to me, and his eyes are so pale that I can see right through them. "What Miss Dovecott saw, she misread. It happens."

"Yeah," I say. "It does."

"You still have her watch?"

"Yeah," I say, "I still have it."

"Keep it," says Glenn. "We're not going to need it."

The Way Boys Read
by Alexander No Middle Name Stromm

There's nothing pretty about it:
they'll claim a book,
brand nicknames to all three sides
as if the book might lose itself in tall grass
or wander, dumb as a cow.
The bookmark? A slice
to the top of the page, unthinking
as a kick to a rock on a dirt road.
And some so quick to break the spine,
the way they've broken girls
with too few words, or with false ones.
If the book is large,
it can be laid flat on a desk
so a boy wouldn't even have to touch it,

just lift a finger to flip a page,
halfheartedly,
like signaling a truck to dump its load.

I ask Miss Dovecott to take a walk with me during lunch, via an invitation scribbled on the back of the poem that I slide under her apartment door. It is time to make my move. This poem is my masterpiece. This one has a title because I approve of its coldhearted truth.

The Way Boys Read

We meet at the head of the running trail. "I liked the poem, Alex," she says. "It may be your best yet."

"It's dark, like me."

"The speaker of the poem and the poet don't have to be one and the same."

And over the hill we go, into the woods.

"I know," I say. "You've taught me that. You've taught me a lot."

There is no one running this time of day. We have the trail to ourselves. Everyone else on campus is feeding themselves. I have to keep the conversation going until we get there, until we get to the place where this is going to happen. But, really, I don't want to talk. I want to throw her down on a bed of leaves and make my mark.

"That's good, Alex. I'm glad. Knowledge is always a silver lining."

I read between the lines of her words, finding justification for what I am about to do. "Speaking of that," I tell her, "we never talked about *In Our Time*." I read the CliffsNotes, not

173

the book, renting them out for a dollar an hour from a future entrepreneur who runs a business out of his dorm room.

"But I thought you couldn't find it in the library," she says.

"Someone had it checked out," I say, "but he returned it."

"So tell me about Nick Adams," she says.

"It's kind of a complicated book, but I guess maybe Hemingway was saying that even after war, there is morality that gives life meaning. After all of that destruction, the purity of the heart still remains. Do you think that was what he was trying to say?"

"I think that's exactly what he was trying to say. I'm impressed."

"The story 'Indian Camp,' that takes place before Nick goes to war, the end of it. It's one of the most perfect things I've ever read."

"Remind me. It's been so long that I've forgotten."

"There's that description of Nick and his father in the boat, the father rowing, the son at the stern, and the sun rising over the hills. Nick lets his hand skim across the water. The morning is cool, but the water is warm."

"Ah, yes." She smiles.

"I memorized the last sentence. 'In the early morning on the lake sitting in the stern of the boat with his father rowing, he felt quite sure that he would never die.'"

"Yes." She nods. "Yes."

"It's what we all think: that we will never die."

She touches my arm with a gentle hand. "But of course we do. It's the one universal experience, other than birth, that we all share."

It is the moment I knew would arrive, when we look at

each other and understand ourselves as equals on the same playing field. Her eyes are wider than I have ever seen them. "Oh, Alex," she whispers, shaking her head, and already, the tears are in her throat. "You will recover from this. You will. Someday."

She takes a step back, leaves rustling for a second, and then, silence in the woods, the loud sound of silence. She is floating away from me, like fog. Because of the tears, she can't see where she's going; there is a large branch fallen across the path, and just as she is about to stumble over it, I dash over, grab her arms, and pull her back toward me. It is all so unreal, fast and slow at the same time, and so strange that I am able, in a moment, to balance and unbalance her.

In a way it feels like the most natural thing in the world when it happens, even though it is planned, even though Glenn is crouched nearby, watching. With my hands on her arms, I draw her into me and keep her there until I have memorized the smell of her hair (pine bark), the scratchiness of her coat (tweed), the heat of her hand on my spine (like a fever). Her own spine is bony, as delicate as a bird's, and when I feel it straighten, I bow to her face and kiss her.

MONDAY, NOVEMBER 20, 7:19 P.M.

Green Fields Gone

Her lips were cold. That surprised me. If I said that she kissed me back, you'd be within your rights to doubt me, but she did. A full kiss, a long one, until she pushed me away with her thin arms, pushed me away, once and for all, which was exactly what I deserved. I flicked a glance at Glenn, whose bottom lip had dropped open in either shock or victory, it

175

was impossible to read. Fear rammed its way into my heart, and this time, I did run as fast as I could. I sprinted up to campus, to the infirmary, and checked myself in for a real-life upset stomach.

Lying there on the bed with the smell of her, the feel of her, all of her words in my head, I felt like the teacher, the one who knew everything. I thought about calling my father to ask him to come get me, to take me skiing, to take me any-where, but I didn't want to have to explain. Instead I spent a very long, very lonely Saturday night wondering if the minute had already passed in which Miss Dovecott had started to hate me.

On Sunday, Miss Dovecott was gone. It was all done qui-etly, her resignation, after Glenn went to Dean Mansfield and told him that he just happened to be running the trail when he saw Miss Dovecott kissing me, a fact that I had to confirm in Mr. Armstrong's office, first with the Headmaster and Mr. Parkes, my advisor, and then over the phone with my father.

So many stories come full circle, and this one does, too: I spent an hour waiting on that bench in the outer hall, wait-ing once again to have my fate handed down to me. I had lied, yes, but only Miss Dovecott knew that for sure, and what I had stolen was metaphorical, not concrete like a can of Coke. And there was nothing in the rule book about students kissing faculty or faculty kissing students. What could they do to me when she was the one who'd initiated it?

Miss Dovecott didn't rat me out for drinking at the scene of the accident. Nor did she rat me out for cheating at hide-and-seek. I had chickened out and hid too close to base, so close that she could never have tagged me. No, she didn't rat me out for anything. Glenn said with a shit-eating smirk that it was because people who live in glass houses know better than to throw stones at their own windows, but I'm not so sure. I would like to believe, in my heart of hearts, that it was selflessness. Miss Dovecott knew for a fact that she'd be fine out there in the real world but that I wouldn't be. She had tried her best to prepare me, but I had offered her irrefutable proof that I wasn't ready for it yet. And so, unselfishly, she let me stay. And selflessness is a kind of love.

But she probably hated me, too. An announcement was made at a special assembly that afternoon that Miss Dovecott had to leave before the year was out because of an illness in her family and that, starting Monday, Mr. McGreavey's wife would take over as our teacher.

TUESDAY, NOVEMBER 21, 7:05 A.M.

Rock

Yesterday was the worst day. The letter I'd been dreading for a month was in my mailbox, which I discovered on my way to track practice. I hurried back to my room to open it in private. You would not believe how violently I was shaking. A folded sheet of monogrammed paper had been signed not only by Thomas's parents, but also by his little brother, Trenton, who had, it appeared, just learned how to write in cursive. That upset me more than anything else, that little wobbly signature.

It was a heartfelt reply, sympathizing with me for having lost a friend and thanking me for being one. They actually apologized for not being able to write sooner. The postscript

177

did its best to abdicate me of any responsibility: *The last thing in the world we want is for you to feel that you could have somehow saved our son.* Which was, of course, exactly how I did feel, how I *should* feel. I laid my head on my desk for hours on end, through track practice, which I skipped and got major demerits for, through the dinner bell and Lights-Out, through what I can without a doubt call, with Robert Frost accuracy, the "darkest evening of the year."

I thought back to the essay that first put me on Miss Dovecott's radar. The last paragraph, like the last sentence of Hemingway's story, I remembered by heart: *What I carry in my backpack down to the river, I carry not knowing that in less than an hour Thomas Broughton will be dead. That is not a knowledge I carry yet, but I will carry it soon—the knowledge of my darkest self—and I will carry it forever.*

TUESDAY, NOVEMBER 28, 9:52 P.M.

Paper Covers Rock

Back from Thanksgiving break, and it's still here, as I knew it would be: my trusty journal, safe behind a whale of a tale that was last checked out in 1964 by Mr. Henley, who has been the head of the English department for a quarter of a century. I have just finished my English essay for tomorrow (yes, the English department gives us homework over Thanksgiving break—thanks, Mr. Henley), so this is it, my last entry, one more attempt to commit the truth to paper. It has not been easy. I have a newfound respect for Mr. Melville, and one day, maybe, I will actually read *Moby-Dick* in its entirety. One day, maybe, I will give this journal back to my dad. But for now, this is where my story belongs until it is time for me to leave this place.

What I record here on the final blank pages of my journal, my confession, my collection of poetry, my collection of guilt, my Not-So-Great American Novel, is this: I am surprised that Miss Dovecott—whose name I have changed (like all names in this whatever-you-want-to-call-it) to protect the innocent—did not mark through the word "forever." She left it hanging there, untainted by red ink. "Forever," a fairy-tale adverb that in some stories spins its magic. And in other stories, like mine, the word stretches itself as thin as a life line. A word burdened with both history and future.

In the end—that is, earlier today—I did talk to Mr. Parkes, mostly because he made me. He wanted to assure me that he and Glenn's advisor were the only faculty members other than Dean Mansfield and Mr. Armstrong who knew what had happened between me and Miss Dovecott. Even though they had debated kicking me out for conduct unbecoming of a Birch student, Mr. Parkes had stood up for me, telling them he thought I had gotten myself caught between a rock and a hard place.

He told me now that he wasn't disappointed in me, and though he never said that he was disappointed in Miss Dovecott, his colleague, I knew he was. In an attempt to make me feel better, he shared bits and pieces from the conversations he had had with her about me, but they only made me feel worse.

Miss Dovecott had admired me for my strength, he said, for the ways that I was learning to know, accept, and heal myself. More than any other student, I had given her hope in what she was doing; because of me, she wasn't teaching to the walls or the air; someone was listening and trying. Someone was aware that through careful arrangements of words, order could be made from chaos. Mr. Parkes even told me that it had given her chills when I'd told her that a poem had come to me while riding the bus back to Birch from a cross-country meet and I hadn't had any paper so I'd written it on the back of a McDonald's napkin in the dark. "You have to stop and freeze the moment," he told me I had told her. "You have to make yourself remember by repeating it in your head over and over. You have to write to preserve your sanity."

When I asked Mr. Parkes why Miss Dovecott had told him all of this, he said there seemed to have been some sort of unspoken vow of solidarity between the two of them to keep tabs on me after Thomas had died. But I wonder if she'd needed Mr. Parkes to keep her in check. In the course of my conversation with Mr. Parkes, her offer to take me to Italy never came up, though maybe it wasn't really an offer. Maybe it was just wishful thinking on my part. Maybe Miss Dovecott in general was wishful thinking on my part. I mean, it's all here—in writing—but as we know by now, stories collide.

In Miss Dovecott's eyes, I was a man among boys: I was a patient student, a patient athlete (I guess she'd gotten that from Mr. Wellfleet), and she'd watched the way I waited tables in the dining hall, never hurried or half-assed. She had observed me eating: I had "elegant" table manners, apparently, and a curious way of bringing my lips to the glass, as if I were a baby bird feeding from its mother. Mr. Parkes said that I was, like Miss Dovecott, an only child, and I will always wonder if there wasn't a dose of narcissism in why she chose me. But I made my English teacher a promise, and even though my faithful reader was no longer here, it was a promise I would keep. It was how I would survive the wreck, after the drama was done.

Mr. Parkes requested that I report to his apartment once a week for hot chocolate and conversation, and once he dismissed me, and with Miss Dovecott's watch in my pocket, I walked to the rock to wait for Glenn. In an hour, we would pay our tribute to Thomas two months after his death. On the bank where he died, we would dig a hole just big enough for the watch and bury it so deep that it would take at least a lifetime for the water to wash it clear. All the rest of my lifetime, without Thomas or Miss Dovecott in it. I knew, standing there, that if Glenn were to ask me to room with him next year, I would say no. But I was pretty sure he wouldn't ask. The burial would mark the end of a lot of things.

When I reached the rock, I climbed up on it. So what if I was breaking a rule? I had broken so many that rules ceased to hold meaning. It was cold, but the sky was blue and clear, the sun so bright that I had to put my hand up as a visor. And then I did something that human beings aren't supposed to do: I stared at the sun without blinking and didn't close my eyes until they burned so hard I couldn't stand it. I opened them to a strange blindness, as if seeing had now become hearing. The water tripped by, but I could still think, I could still understand. Flattening my back onto the cold stone, I took deep breaths and let the sun trace, like chalk at a crime scene, the outline of my body.

Acknowledgments

It does indeed take a village. I would like to extend my most heartfelt thanks to

Kathi Appelt, my guardian angel, for her impressive wingspan.

Jonathan Lyons, my invaluable agent, for giving my voice a voice.

Michelle Poploff, my editor, for settling on me and then not settling.

Rebecca Short, editorial assistant, for her sharp, young eyes.

Ben Hale and Ted Blain, for investing their wisdom in my words.

Sally Hawn, my sister and first reader always.

My sister Leigh Hubbard and my brother-in-law Andy Evans, best possible audience for my boarding-school stories.

Jayne and Joel Hubbard, for reading to me before I knew how.

Steve Cobb, for so much in my life that is good and true.